Michael Pearce grew [up in the] Sudan among the va[rious peoples of the] Mamur Zapt series. [He later returned] to teach, and retains a huma[n rights] interest in the area. In between whiles, his career has followed the standard academic rake's progress from teaching to writing to editing to administration. He finds international politics a pallid imitation of academic ones. He lives in London.

This is his eleventh Mamur Zapt novel; the twelfth in the series, *Death of an Effendi*, is available in hardcover from Collins Crime. Michael Pearce is the winner of the Crime Writers' Association's Last Laugh Award for Funniest Crime Novel of the Year for *The Mamur Zapt and the Spoils of Egypt*.

He is also the author of the acclaimed Dmitri Kameron crime series, set in Tsarist Russia.

Praise for Michael Pearce

'This series continues to be the most delightful in current detective fiction'   *Gerald Kaufman, Scotsman*

'Pearce … takes apart ancient history and reassembles it with beguiling wit and colour'   *Sunday Times*

'Irresistible fun'   *Time Out*

'The Mamur Zapt's sly, irreverent humour continues to refresh the parts others seldom reach'   *Observer*

By the same author

DEATH OF AN EFFENDI
THE FIG TREE MURDER
THE MINGRELIAN CONSPIRACY
THE SNAKE-CATCHER'S DAUGHTER
THE MAMUR ZAPT AND THE CAMEL OF DESTRUCTION
THE MAMUR ZAPT AND THE SPOILS OF EGYPT
THE MAMUR ZAPT AND THE GIRL IN THE NILE
THE MAMUR ZAPT AND THE MEN BEHIND
THE MAMUR ZAPT AND THE DONKEY-VOUS
THE MAMUR ZAPT AND THE NIGHT OF THE DOG
THE MAMUR ZAPT AND THE RETURN OF THE CARPET

MICHAEL PEARCE

THE LAST CUT

A Mamur Zapt mystery

HarperCollinsPublishers

This novel is entirely a work of fiction. The names, characters and incidents portrayed in it are the work of the author's imagination. Any resemblance to actual persons, living or dead, events or localities is entirely coincidental.

HarperCollins*Publishers*
77–85 Fulham Palace Road,
Hammersmith, London W6 8JB

The HarperCollins website address is:
www.**fire**and**water**.com

This paperback edition 2000

1 3 5 7 9 8 6 4 2

First published in Great Britain by
HarperCollins*Publishers* 1998

Copyright © Michael Pearce 1998

Michael Pearce asserts the moral right to
be identified as the author of this work

ISBN 0 00 651081 7

Set in Meridien and Bodoni

Printed and bound in Great Britain by
Caledonian International Book Manufacturing Ltd, Glasgow

All rights reserved. No part of this publication may be reproduced, stored in a retrieval system, or transmitted, in any form or by any means, electronic, mechanical, photocopying, recording or otherwise, without the prior permission of the publishers.

This book is sold subject to the condition that it shall not, by way of trade or otherwise, be lent, re-sold, hired out or otherwise circulated without the publisher's prior consent in any form of binding or cover other than that in which it is published and without a similar condition including this condition being imposed on the subsequent purchaser.

1

'It will be for the last time,' said Garvin, the Commandant of Police.

'It seems a pity,' said the Kadi's representative, 'after a thousand years.'

'Oh, more than that,' said McPhee, the Deputy Commandant. 'The rites almost certainly antedate the Arab invasion. The ancient Egyptians –'

'Yes, well, thank you,' said Garvin. 'That all?'

'There's the question of the gravediggers,' said the young man from the Consulate.

'Gravediggers?'

'Yes. The ones who actually make the cut. It's either the Muslim gravediggers or the Jews. This year it's the Jews.'

'Well, then –'

'Yes, but it falls on their Sabbath this year.'

'Okay, let the Muslim gravediggers do it, then.'

'They won't like that!'

'The Muslims?'

'No, the Jews. It's their turn.'

'Yes, but they won't do it on the Sabbath, I thought you said?'

'Well, they will do it if they're told to. And if they get paid extra.'

There was a little silence.

'I suppose I could get the Old Man to talk to the Finance Department.'

'And I could get the Kadi to talk to the Khedive and get him to tell them.'

'That all settled, then? Nothing else?' asked Garvin. 'Right, Mamur Zapt, the rest is up to you.'

As they got up from the table, McPhee said:

'They used to sacrifice a maiden, you know.'

'Nonsense!' said the Kadi's representative. 'That's just a myth. Anyway, it was the Christians.'

'That's a myth, too,' said the representative of the Copts hastily. 'You can't blame it on us. The Canal wasn't built till the Arabs came.'

'The rite may be older,' said McPhee. 'It almost certainly dates back to the Pharaohs.'

'Let's blame them, then,' said the young man from the Consulate, picking up his papers. 'At least they can't answer back.'

'That's all in the past, anyway,' said Garvin. 'These days we've got other things to think about.'

'What other things?' asked Owen. It was the first time he'd done this.

'Oh, the general disorder. People use it as an excuse –'

'They certainly do,' said McPhee, cheeks going pink.

'To do what?'

'Well . . .'

'The women go unveiled, that sort of thing,' said the Kadi's representative.

'Worse than that,' said McPhee primly.

'Really?' said Owen. 'Exactly what –?'

'You'll find out,' said Garvin. 'At any rate, it will be for the last time.'

'Watch out for the Maiden,' said the young man from the Consulate, as he and Owen left the room together.

They found her, of course, the next day.

The canal bed, awaiting the water, was dry now throughout most of its insalubrious length. It ran through the heart of the city from Old Cairo to the new barracks at Abbasiya and was a handy dumping-place for rubbish of all kinds, from excrement to onion peelings to collapsed angarib rope-beds to dead dogs; and, of course, to dead humans. It had the additional advantage in the last case that towards the time

6

of the Inundation it had become so foul as to deter all but the lowest scavengers from venturing into it. The maiden would have gone undiscovered had it not been for the fact that the ceremonial cutting of the dam involved the construction of a tall cone of earth, and it was while the workmen had been working on this that they had come upon the body.

Bodies deteriorated quickly in the heat and it was by no means evident now that the body *was* that of a maiden, but the workmen were in no doubt. Nor, unfortunately, was the rest of the population of Cairo.

'Blast it!' said Garvin. 'They'll all connect it with ending the Cut!'

Every year when the waters of the Nile began to rise, a temporary dam was constructed across the mouth of the Khalig Canal, just opposite Roda Island. When the Nilometer on the Island showed that the water was at its highest, the dam was cut and the water allowed to flow through the canal. The moment traditionally marked the release of waters throughout the land, when the dams would be opened and the water pour into the canals and through the irrigation system as a whole.

After this year the water would still pour but the Cut would be no more. The canal was to be filled in and a tramway put on top of it.

All the Departments were pleased: Sanitation, because the canal was a notorious health hazard, Transport, because they got a new tramway out of it, Finance, because they got it at a cost of next to nothing, Irrigation, because the damned thing was an irrelevance anyway, the Government generally because it could be seen as modernization.

The ordinary Cairene, however, who had always had great affection for the festivities which accompanied the Cut, was much less happy.

'The British are taking away all our pleasures,' they grumbled.

In most countries they would have blamed the Government. In Egypt they blamed the British. This was reasonable since the British ran the country. Invited in by a former Khedive to assist him to straighten out the country's finances, they had decided to assist him to straighten out a few other things as well, and were still, thirty years later, assisting.

'Another example of the British killjoy spirit!' thundered the popular (Arab) press. 'First, they ban the Hoseini celebrations –'

'But that was because they were mutilating each other!' protested Owen.

It had been the practice, as part of the general festivity, for dervishes to slash each other with swords, scourge their backs with razor-like chains, and impale themselves, and their neighbours, on meat-hooks.

'Surely you don't defend –' he had said to his friend, Mahmoud.

Mahmoud, a young lawyer in the Ministry of Justice, was the last person to defend such practices. He regarded them as a thing of the past and the past was exactly what he wanted to get rid of. Like most of the Ministry lawyers, he was a member of the Nationalist Party and committed to modernization. For that reason he wasn't much in favour of the canal, either.

'It's an open sewer,' he said.

Nevertheless, he felt sorry about the ending of the Cut.

If even he, arch-modernizer that he was, felt a twinge over the Cut's going, then Owen could just imagine how the ordinary inhabitants of the city felt. The Cut was part of popular history. Removing it was like removing a part of oneself, a tooth, say, yes, a wisdom tooth, useless but painful to extract. Not only that; some people believed in the wisdom. They might resist its going.

That was why this time Owen had become involved. Ordinarily, marshalling the festivity was a matter of simple policing and Owen preferred to leave simple policing to the simple police. The Mamur Zapt, Head of what had in the past been known as the Khedive's Secret Police and what was today very properly thought of, in English terms, as the Political Branch, had a more discreet responsibility for preserving law and order. The Khedive liked to say that the Mamur Zapt was the hidden hand that held the city. Rather too often he saw the hand as a fist; whereas Owen preferred to keep it hidden.

What concerned him now was that whereas in any normal city the ending of the Cut would be merely a matter for mutter, in the explosive mixture of races and religions that was Cairo it could very quickly and all too easily ignite into violence. And the Maiden was just the thing that could provide the spark.

About the Maiden as maiden, Owen, as Mamur Zapt, cared nothing at all. Ordinary murder was not his concern. But about the Maiden as a possible source of political conflagration he cared a great deal. Even if she was a myth.

Which was why he decided to take an interest in the case. He rang up the Parquet to ask who was handling it.

'El Zaki,' they said.

This was fortunate, for El Zaki was Owen's friend, Mahmoud.

'Where is he?' he asked.

'At the mortuary.'

This was fortunate, too, as the mortuary was the only cool place in Cairo. He went there with speed, or, at least, in an arabeah, the horse-drawn cab which at that time in Cairo served as taxi. Unsurprisingly, this being August, when men, flowers and horses drooped, by the time he got there Mahmoud was coming out.

'Do they serve coffee in there?'

'Yes, but it smells of formaldehyde.'

They went instead to a café round the corner. It was an Arab café and, as in most Arab cafés, the main room was underground, where darkness provided relief from the sun.

'So they've put you on this?'

'Yes,' said Mahmoud ruefully. 'You can't win them all.'

'I'd like to take an interest.'

'No one else is,' said Mahmoud sourly. 'Not at the Parquet, at any rate.'

The Parquet was the Department of Prosecutions at the Ministry of Justice, to which Mahmoud belonged. In Egypt criminal investigation was not the responsibility of the police. Their task was merely to notify the Parquet that a crime had been committed. Once that had been done, responsibility for conducting the investigation was, as in the French system on which the Egyptian system was based, with the lawyer the Parquet assigned to the case.

'I hope you're right about that.'

He told Mahmoud of his fears. Mahmoud dismissed them.

'The body could have been dumped anywhere,' he said.

'Yes. I know. But people are making a connection with the Cut.'

Mahmoud had little time for myths and none at all for the Myth of the Maiden.

'Superstitious nonsense,' he said. 'We're not still in the Dark Age, you know.'

Owen thought that some Egyptians, the ones he was worried about, might be dragging their feet. He wisely kept silent, however. Mahmoud was inclined to be touchy about remarks which he considered reflected upon Egypt.

'What does the autopsy show?' he asked.

'The report's not ready yet. It's taking a while because of the condition of the body. There is some evidence of deterioration through water. If that turns out to be true, it would help us to establish when the body was dumped. There was still water in the Canal. That would put it in March or April.'

'Or later,' said Owen. 'Even when most of it's dry, there are still stagnant pools. Have you established the cause of death?'

'Impossible to tell yet. Some evidence of wounding to the lower abdominal region. But that could just have been dogs.'

'No evidence of, well, wounding of a ritual nature?'

'I don't know what that would be,' said Mahmoud coldly. 'We don't have ritual killings in Cairo. Now, if we were some obscure tribe down in the Sudan –'

'All right, all right. I don't know what it would be, either. But if we could rule it out publicly, that might help to dispel the myth –'

'She could have died of old age for all we can tell at the moment,' said Mahmoud. 'And it's about time the Myth of the Maiden did.'

Owen, wisely, let the matter drop.

*   *   *

10

'Failed?' said the engineer from the Irrigation Department. 'Our regulators don't fail!'

'Regulator?' said Owen. 'What's a régulator?'

'You don't know what a regulator is! It's a – well –'

'It's like a gate,' said the Under-Secretary, to whose office Owen had been frantically summoned. 'A gate in a dam. It controls the flow of water through the dam.'

'And it's failed? Well, I'm sorry about that. But, look, it all sounds very technical to me. I don't quite see why I've been –'

'It's *not* failed!' cried the engineer in exasperation. 'That's what I keep trying to say! It's been sabotaged!'

The Manufiyah Regulator was one of the huge series of works which together formed the Delta Barrage. The barrage was built across the Nile about fifteen miles north of Cairo just where the river divided into two great arms which continued independently to the Mediterranean, coming out at Rosetta and Damietta. It controlled the supply of water to the whole of Lower Egypt but in particular to the immensely fertile region that lay between the arms. It distributed the water through a number of canals, the flow in each of which was determined by a separate regulator. The Manufiyah Regulator was one of the most important of these.

'Important?' said the Under-Secretary, who was travelling with them in the Irrigation Department's launch. 'You'd think so if you were a farmer in the Middle Delta!'

Owen could see the barrage now, rising up ahead of them. It was like a long castellated wall, with minarets in the centre and a campanile at each end. As it came closer, he could make out the arches, a hundred and thirty of them altogether, the engineer said. He looked for the damage.

'No, no!' said the engineer impatiently. 'Not there! Behind! Regulator. Canal. See?'

That was exactly what Owen didn't see. What he did see, suddenly, away to his right, was a vision of palms and water: palms jutting up from the water as from tiny islands in a sea; men walking between the islands apparently on the surface

11

of the water but actually on little earth walls; buffaloes forging contentedly through the shallows but every now and then, surprised, dropping suddenly and having to swim, with their great noses held up high out of the water; flat, punt-like boats poled along by a man, often with a little boy in the stern, holding an animal, a calf or a goat, by the front hooves as it splashed behind, exactly as in the ancient friezes.

The vision shimmered and he knew that it wasn't there really, or, rather, that it was not there but somewhere else, not there in the desert where he was looking but somewhere else, down river, where the water had already spread over the fields.

He turned to the engineer.

'You've already released it, then?'

'Some of it. It seemed best, with one of the regulators going. But we would have released it anyway.'

'Without waiting for the Cut?'

'Cut? What's that? Oh, I know, the Khalig Canal and all that stuff. No, that's all in the past. We don't wait for that nowadays. No, it's nothing to do with us.'

The single long wall of the barrage was in a sense illusory. There were, in fact, two separate barrages, one across the Damietta arm of the Nile, the other across the Rosetta arm. Each barrage was about five hundred metres long and they were linked by a revetment wall which ran for a thousand metres over the triangle of ground between the arms. The triangle had been made into spectacular gardens which were a great draw to the city's inhabitants at weekends and on festival days.

Today, of course, there was an even greater draw and the Gardens on the Rosetta side were a solid mass of people. Policemen had to force a way through for the Minister and his party.

They were also trying, rather less successfully, to clear a passage for a long line of carts piled high with rubble, stretching now right across the Gardens. As each cart came up to the damaged regulator, it was turned and then backed up on to the embankment which led to the small service road running across the top of the regulator gates. It was then edged along the road until it reached the gap, where it would discharge its load in a great crash of stone and spray.

It was the turning of the carts that was the problem. The people were wedged in so tightly at that point that the carts could hardly make inroads. The drivers lost patience and laid about them with their whips, the constables with their batons. The crowd did not, could not budge.

'Clear the bloody lot out of the way!' shouted a furious voice from down at the foot of the regulator somewhere.

Constables, carts, workmen and sympathetic onlookers hurled themselves at the crowd. It gave a yard or two. Some small boys fell into the river. Other onlookers were forced on to the flower beds.

'My beds! My beds!' cried an anguished voice.

A stocky little man, galabeeyah skirts hitched up round his knees, skull cap askew on his head, rushed across desperately.

'Have you no thought? Have you no sense? Have you no feeling?'

He hammered on the sides of a cart with his fists.

The driver, face running with sweat, glanced down.

'Abdullah, there are more important things in life just now than bougainvillea!'

He struck the horse a mighty blow with his whip. It shot forward, across a rose-bed and into a clump of datura, where it stuck. The heavy white blossoms closed over its flanks like ornamental wreaths.

'I shall kill it!' cried the gardener wildly, seizing a spade.

Concerned onlookers seized *him*.

'But, Abdullah,' one of them remonstrated, 'the water is important –'

The gardener stopped his struggling. 'Water?' he said. 'Do you think you need to tell me about water? Me? How do you think all this grows, then? What do you think I –?'

Owen moved away. If there was one thing any Egyptian was guaranteed to have a view on, it was water.

Which made it all the more extraordinary that –

* * *

13

The Ministerial party had at last reached the regulator. Down at its foot, some in the water, some out, men were working frantically. Among them was a European in a helmet. He looked up, then scrambled up to meet them.

'Hello, Minister! Glad to see you!'

'How are you getting on?'

The helmeted man shrugged.

'At the moment we're just trying to get it under control,' he said.

'Any idea of the extent of the damage?'

'One of the gates has gone.'

He pointed to the regulator. The gates had been forced open. One of them bent back at an angle.

'It got the full force of the blast.'

'It definitely was a blast, was it?' asked Owen.

The man looked at him.

'Owen, is it? The Mamur Zapt? Seen you at the Club, but not spoken. Glad to meet you.' They shook hands. 'Yes, it definitely was. I can show you. Not just this moment, though. I've got things I must –'

He glanced back at the regulator.

'No, that's fine. Look, I won't take your time. Can you put me on to someone else? Anyone see anything? Presumably you yourself weren't –'

'I was in bed. It was two o'clock in the morning.'

'Someone called you. Who was that?'

'The watchman. Ahmed.'

'Can I have a word with him? Where would I find him?'

The engineer pointed up to the main wall of the barrage.

'He's up there,' he said. 'Ask for Ahmed.'

The watchman's hut was empty except for a woman with a baby and a small boy. When Owen asked for Ahmed, she nodded and sent the boy to fetch him. Meanwhile, Owen walked out on to the barrage.

Upstream, feluccas were tacking gracefully in the wind and, closer to, a large gyassa, sails newly lowered and rigging bright with the little scarlet flags used for marriages and the return of pilgrims from Mecca, was disgorging passengers on

14

to the shore. They were already beginning to make their way up to the gardens, past a long line of stalls selling peanuts and pastries and sweetmeats and souvenirs. In the gardens there were yet more stalls, tucked among the bamboo thickets and the prickly pears, the clumps of datura and the bright masses of bougainvillea.

Everywhere, too, there were water-sellers. It was a hot day and their services were much in demand; so much so that there was a steady file of them going back to the river to replenish their water-skins. Down by the gyassa he could see their black bags floating on the water.

The boy returned with an old, grey-haired man; not too old, apparently, for both the boy and the baby were his.

'Pardon my slowness, Effendi.'

'Even the Khedive should wait for age,' said Owen courteously.

'Ah, it's not age,' said the man, tapping his leg. 'It's this. I broke it when we were building the Dam at Aswan. It set badly and they said I could not work again. But when Macrae Effendi came up here he sent for me and made me watchman.'

'And you were watching last night?'

'That is so.'

'And what did you see?'

The man hesitated.

'Well, Effendi, it was not what I saw. It was – I was out on the bridge. And then the air hissed suddenly across my face and at once there was a mighty clap, as of thunder. And I said: "That cannot be right, for no one does that sort of work at night." For I knew what it was, having worked on the Dam at Aswan. And then I heard the rush of water, and saw the whiteness in the darkness, and knew the dam had broken. And I hastened back and sounded the signal and called Macrae Effendi.'

'You did well.'

'And then I went back on to the bridge. Effendi, I know I could have gone to the breach. But with this –' he motioned towards his leg – 'what could I have done? And, besides, Macrae Effendi says: "Let every man do his duty. If every man does his duty, then all will be well." And my duty, Effendi, was on the bridge.'

'Quite right. So there you were, back on the bridge, watching, as was your duty. What else did you see?'

'Nothing, Effendi. The night was dark. But shortly I heard shouts and knew that the workmen were there. And then I heard Macrae Effendi.'

'But you saw nothing? No man fleeing the spot, for instance?'

'It was dark, Effendi. And, besides, he would have come through the gardens, where there are trees and bushes.'

'There are other watchmen?'

'There are watchmen on all the dams when the river rises. But, Effendi, they would have been watching the dams and the banks.'

'They would have been watching against the river and not against people?'

'That is right. What need is there to watch against people? To strike against the river is to strike against oneself.'

'And yet last night someone did.'

'What could have possessed them, Effendi?' asked the watchman, shaking his head. 'Who could do a thing like that?'

'Some loony,' said Macrae bitterly, now unhelmeted and slumped exhaustedly in the office. There was coffee on the table in front of them. He picked up one of the cups.

'Inexplicable!' said the Minister. 'Unless –' he looked at Owen – 'you don't think it could have been some ridiculous Nationalist –?'

'Politics, you mean?' said Macrae. 'Well, you could be right. Anyone who gets mixed up with politics has to be crazy. Especially in Egypt. Oh, sorry, Minister!'

'Let's not jump to conclusions!' said Owen. 'It could just be an individual with a grudge.'

'Well, let's hope you find him before he does any more damage,' said Macrae.

'Are you going to be able to put this right?' the Minister asked.

'Depends what you mean. We'll have things more or less under control by the evening. But then we'll need new gates.'

'New gates?'

'And we'll have to set them,' said the other engineer, the one Owen had met at the Ministry. His name was Ferguson. 'That means that what we're talking about really is a complete new regulator.'

'But that will cost millions!' said the Minister.

'Aye,' said Macrae.

'We'll have to divert the canal,' said Ferguson.

'Divert the canal!'

'Aye,' said Macrae.

'But – but – that will –'

'Cost more millions,' said Ferguson.

'We have to keep the flow going, you see,' said Macrae. 'And you can't build when the water's still going through. You have to build somewhere else. Nearby, of course.' He looked out of the window. 'The gardens, I should think. And then divert the water into the new channel.'

The Under-Secretary pulled himself together.

'I'll put it to them. It – it may take some time.'

'Can't wait,' said Macrae. Ferguson nodded in agreement. 'If you want it done before next year's rise – and you do – you'll have to start next month.'

'I'll put that to them, too,' said the Under-Secretary, downcast.

'But that's not the main thing,' said Macrae.

'No?' said the Under-Secretary.

'No?' said Ferguson, surprised.

'No. The main thing is to get the madman who did it. Before he does it again. Owen?'

2

The world of water, on the brink of which Owen had hitherto
remained, was clearly a different one from any that he had
known. It seemed, for a start, to be inhabited primarily
by Scotsmen. Owen put this down to the fact that it was
technical. He had long established that all engineers, in the
Levant at any rate, were Scottish. It must be something
in the blood, he decided; which perhaps accounted for him
himself having no technical competence whatsoever. He
understood enough about such things, however, to know
when someone was being given the technical run-around.
As here, he suspected.

After the Minister had left, shell-shocked, Macrae produced a bottle of whisky and three glasses.

'Do you like it with water or without?'

Owen hesitated.

'Aye,' said Macrae, 'you're right. It's a big question. I take
it with just a splash, myself. It releases the aromas.'

'Aye, but that's in Scotland,' said Ferguson. 'Out here,
where it's warmer, they're released anyway.'

'You don't take it with ice, anyway. That's the main thing,'
said Macrae, pouring a generous dram.

'In the Club, perhaps. With soda. And a different whisky.'

'My view entirely,' said Macrae. He took a careful sip,
nodded approval, and put his glass down.

'Now,' he said, 'you'll have some questions for us, I
fancy.'

'Basic facts, first,' said Owen.

'Aye,' said Macrae. 'I like facts.'

'First: time?'

'A couple of minutes either side of two o'clock. Ahmed phoned me at five past. I was here by twenty past.'

'Good.'

'Next, place. You'll be wanting to know about that. Well,'– he looked at Ferguson for corroboration – 'I'd say bottom right-hand corner of the gates as you look towards the main barrage. About by the culvert.'

'Aye,' said Ferguson. 'We'll be able to tell you better later.'

'What was it done with?' asked Owen.

'Dynamite, I fancy,' said Macrae. 'Where there's dams, there's dynamite. Have you checked the store?' he asked Ferguson.

'Not yet,' said Ferguson. 'I will.'

'They'll have come across the Gardens,' said Owen. 'I'll take a look at those in a moment.'

'You won't find anything,' said Ferguson. 'They're a labyrinth.'

'I'll look, anyway. Now I want to ask you about workmen.'

'Workmen?' said Macrae, surprised. 'Why?'

'One of them could have done it.'

Macrae and Ferguson both shook their heads.

'Not one of ours,' they said in unison.

'Why not?'

'Well –' Macrae sat back and thought. 'We've known them for years,' he said finally. 'Some of them worked with me down at Aswan.'

'Even the ones who come up for the Inundation,' said Ferguson. 'We've known them for years. Every year, there they are. Really, there are too many of them. I ought to turn some away. They're needed elsewhere in the system. But we know them and they know us.'

'Good men,' said Macrae.

'What, all of them?' said Owen.

'Look,' said Macrae. 'I know what they say about Egyptian workmen. But ours are not like that.'

'All of them?' said Owen. 'I'm looking for one, that's the point.'

'We'd have got rid of them if they were.'

19

'Well, that, too, could be the point.'

'What are you saying?'

'I'm asking, not saying. I'm asking why anyone would want to do a thing like this. And the answer I come up with is: because they've got a grudge.'

'Grudge?' said Ferguson. 'Who against?'

'The Department. You.'

'Not our workmen,' said Macrae positively. 'Why would they have a grudge?'

'Because they fancied they'd been wronged. Let's have a try. Any injuries lately?'

'Nothing serious. It's not construction work. It's not like Aswan. And when there are injuries we look after them.'

'But you do have injuries?'

'Yes, but –'

'I'd like the names. Next, dismissals.'

'We don't have any.'

'You said yourself that if people weren't up to the mark you got rid of them.'

'Yes. But – Look, all that is in the past. We haven't needed to get rid of anyone for –'

'Years,' filled in Ferguson.

'What about disciplinary problems? Don't tell me you haven't had any of those!'

'If we have, we've known how to handle them.'

'But that's the point: *how* they were handled.'

'Look –'

'We've had words,' said Ferguson. 'I don't deny that. But nothing serious.'

'Blows?'

'I don't believe in blows,' said Macrae. 'If you can't manage without blows, you can't manage.'

'Fine!' said Owen. 'But let me have the names, will you?'

'The Department's got the records,' said Ferguson.

'In any case,' said Macrae, 'aren't you barking up the wrong tree? If they had a grudge against us, wouldn't they want to take it out on us? Not on a dam they depend on for their

20

livelihood. The only people they'd be hurting there would be themselves!'

Out by the damaged regulator the crowds were thinning now and the carts could turn more easily. They were still coming. The long line still stretched across the gardens. It was testimony to the engineers' capacity for getting things done that they had been able to organize so many loads in such a short space of time.

The loads, inevitably, were an incongruous mixture. There was masonry, rubble, rocks, wood, mattresses – even old chairs and tables. Not so old, as a matter of fact. Some of them were quite new.

'Mr Macrae said anything would do,' explained the hot young man marshalling the carts. His pinkness told that he was fresh from England. 'He said that I could raid the houses if necessary. A lot of them are just standing empty, you know.'

A cart went by piled high with swathes of fine velvet curtaining. On top teetered a beautiful old escritoire.

'Just a minute –' said Owen.

'Where did you get that?' asked Ferguson.

'Oh, a sort of villa over there,' said the young man, pointing along the river bank.

'But –' said Ferguson.

'Anything wrong?' inquired the pink youth anxiously.

'That's the Khedive's Summer Chalet,' said Owen.

'Murderers!' muttered the gardener wrathfully, struggling to restore a rose-bed.

'Take heart, man,' counselled Owen, standing beside him. 'The people will go, the gardens remain.'

'But what will they be like?' asked the gardener.

'In time they will be as new.'

'Ah, yes,' said the gardener, 'but how much time? A garden like this isn't built in a day, you know.'

'It takes time,' agreed Owen soothingly.

'And work! A garden is built with one's back.'

'But out of the sweat of one's brow a thing of beauty emerges.'

'Well –'

'This is truly one of the Wonders of Egypt,' said Owen, looking round.

'Well –' said the gardener modestly.

'Of Egypt? No, of the world!'

'It's pretty good,' acknowledged the gardener. 'Though I say it myself.'

'Who better to say it?'

'And those stupid bastards –'

'Yes, yes,' said Owen hurriedly. 'But, tell me, Abdullah, you of all men must know the gardens well?'

'Like the back of my hand.'

'Just so. And you will be able to tell me this: if you were coming by night and making for the Manufiya Regulator, and did not wish to be seen, by what way would you come?'

The gardener gave him a shrewd look.

'Would you be carrying something, Effendi?'

'You might. You might well.'

'Then there is only one way you would come. For if you came by any other you would have to cross canals. And you would not want, would you, Effendi, to get your load wet?'

'You would not. So how would you come?'

'Shall I show you, Effendi?'

Owen was not exactly a connoisseur of gardens. Indeed, he seldom noticed that they were there at all. But even he, now that he looked, could see that there was something special about the Barrage Gardens. They were a miracle of colour. Everywhere there were great splashes of bougainvillea and datura, banks of roses, huge beds of thrift. The trees, many of them rare and not native to Egypt, were tied together with flowering creepers and lianas. The pools, and there were lots of pools, were vivid with the ancient emblems of Lower and Upper Egypt, the papyrus and the lotos.

The gardens occupied the land between the Rosetta and Damietta arms of the Nile which was completely flat. That was not, however, the impression you received as you walked through them. Every rise, every declivity, had been somehow enhanced so that what you were conscious of, unusually in Egypt, was wooded hills and valleys.

22

It was along one of these valleys that Abdullah was leading Owen. A stream ran down the middle and on the opposite side were crumbling walls festooned with brightly-coloured climbers, the remains of the old French fort which had been here. Scattered along the valley were great clumps of bamboo and prickly pear, all making, thought Owen, if you wanted it, for invisibility.

He saw now that they were coming to the edge of the gardens. For the whole of their walk they had been out of sight of the barrages; out of sight, too, he suddenly realized, of any of the watchmen who might be manning them.

Except that –

'Hello, Ibrahim!' said the gardener.

A man was lying on his back beneath a baobab tree, an antique musket stretched out alongside him.

'He sleeps during the day,' said the gardener with a grin, 'because he works during the night. Or so he claims.'

'He is, then –?'

'The ghaffir.'

The night watchman. He sat up, yawned and splashed water over his face from a nearby gadwal.

'I am showing this Effendi how a man might get to the Manufiya Regulator without being seen,' said the gardener.

'You are showing him the wrong way, then,' said the ghaffir, 'for if he had come this way, I would have seen him.'

'Not during the night, Ibrahim. For would you not have been walking the gardens?'

'I might still have seen him,' said the ghaffir, 'if he had walked this way. For that is the way I walk when I am going to see that the stores are all right.'

'And did you in fact see anyone?' asked Owen. 'Or anything untoward?'

The ghaffir chuckled.

'I saw no one, Effendi. But I did see something untoward.'

'What was that?'

'Well, I didn't really see it, Effendi. Unfortunately. But I heard.'

'What did you hear?'

23

'Chuckling, Effendi.'

'Chuckling?'

'And other noises, Effendi.' He winked knowingly. 'As of lovers.'

'And you saw them, Ibrahim?' said the gardener, scandalized.

'Not actually saw them. They were in the bushes.'

'And you're sure about the noises?' asked Owen. 'I mean, that they were –?'

'Effendi, they were like a pair of jackals!'

'Ibrahim!' said the gardener, shocked, but delighted.

'Like this!'

The ghaffir gave an orgiastic cry.

'Okay, okay,' said Owen. 'And where did all this take place?'

'Just there, Effendi,' said the ghaffir, pointing. 'I had just got back from the stores when I heard –'

'Ibrahim!'

'All right, all right. And you saw, or heard, nothing else?'

'No, Effendi. But that was pretty good, wasn't it?'

'I'll bet he had a look,' said the gardener, as they walked back to the regulator.

At the regulator the men were taking a break. They were sprawled tiredly on the bank.

'Hard work!' said Owen sympathetically.

'It's what we're paid for,' said one of the men.

'If this is what we're going to do all day,' said the man next to him, 'then I'm not being paid enough!'

'You'd rather be back at home, would you, Musa?' asked someone, apparently innocently.

There was a general laugh.

'I don't know about that,' said Musa.

'It's his wife,' someone explained to Owen. 'She keeps him on the go.'

'You'd better make the most of it while you've got the chance, Musa,' said someone else. 'You'll be back there soon enough.'

'If this gate business doesn't hold things back,' said Musa.

The men turned serious.

'You don't think it'll come to that?'

'We wouldn't want that,' said someone. 'There's work to be done at home.'

'You're just up here for the Inundation, are you?' asked Owen.

'That's right. It works out very well usually. There's not much we can do at home just now. At this time of year you've got to wait for the water. And then when it comes you've got to wait for it to sink in before you can plant the seed. By that time we're home again.'

'You work your own lands, do you?'

There was a rueful chuckle.

'It's mostly Al-Sayyid Hannam's land now. But, yes, we work it.'

'They're fellahin,' said Ferguson, joining him. 'They work in the fields. Every man jack of them. And if there's anyone who knows the meaning of water, it's the Egyptian fellah. That's why I can't believe it would be one of them. I just can't!'

The workmen started to go back. Macrae was already there. He saw Owen and waved an arm in greeting. Owen suddenly realized that the man had been there since two o'clock the previous night. He wondered if the workmen had, too. They were going back to work, however, willingly enough.

Ferguson squinted at the sun.

'I'd better be rigging up some lights,' he said.

The sun was already beginning its downward plunge. The Egyptian twilight was short. Already there was a reddish tinge to the water.

The gardens were emptying rapidly.

'You'd best be getting back,' said Ferguson.

Owen joined the crowd streaming back down to the river on the other side of the main barrage. Down at the water's edge the boats were filling up fast. The big gyassa had already left. There was no sign of the launch. He found a felucca which was not too crowded and stepped in.

*   *   *

25

By the time the felucca nosed into the bank at Bulaq, the sun had already set and the lights were coming on in the streets. He took an arabeah back to the Bab-el-Khalk, the Police Headquarters, where he had his office. There were no lights in that. Like all Government buildings it closed for the day at two. Admittedly it opened at seven.

He found a porter, however, who produced a lamp and showed him to his office. He wasn't going to stay, he merely wanted to check for messages. There was one from Mahmoud suggesting a meeting. The first findings of the autopsy had come through.

Owen knew Mahmoud's habits. Indeed, they were his own and those of most Cairenes. After the inertia of the afternoon the city came alive in the evening and made for the cafés. Owen tried one or two of Mahmoud's favourites and found him at a third. He was sitting outside at a table, sipping coffee and preparing for an appearance in court tomorrow.

'I tried to get you earlier,' he said.

'I was up at the barrage.'

'The regulator?'

'Yes.' Then, knowing that Mahmoud would be wondering, he said: 'It looks like sabotage.'

'Sabotage?' said Mahmoud, surprised. 'But who on earth would –?'

'Exactly,' said Owen. He asked about the autopsy.

'They're only preliminary findings,' said Mahmoud, 'but I thought you'd be interested.'

The Maiden, it appeared, had not been murdered at all, ritually or otherwise, but had died of natural causes.

'If you can call it that,' said Mahmoud.

'Why shouldn't you call it that?'

'She probably died as a result of circumcision.'

'It went wrong?'

'That, or infection.'

As was commonly the case. The practice was widespread, especially in the older, poorer and more traditional quarters of the city. It was defended on the grounds of hygiene but the operation itself often took place in circumstances that were the reverse of hygienic, performed by an old woman

26

in a filthy room, with consequences that were too frequently the same as those in the case of the Maiden.

Owen was silent for a moment, then shrugged.

'Well,' he said, 'in a way that's quite helpful for me at any rate. Any chance that we could publish the findings?'

'Why not?' said Mahmoud.

'It would help me if we could. It would knock all the daft "Myth of the Maiden" nonsense on the head. And with the Cut coming up so soon –'

'I don't see why not,' said Mahmoud. 'I'd have to make it clear that they were preliminary findings, of course.'

'They're not likely to be altered, though, are they?'

'I wouldn't have thought so. Only if something new comes up. Or if they find anything unusual. Actually,' said Mahmoud, 'there *is* something unusual. Mildly so. Her age. Circumcision usually takes place at thirteen, or even younger. This girl was about twenty.'

'That's not going to affect anything, though, is it?'

'No. I just find it puzzling, that's all.'

'A late marriage, perhaps?'

'Perhaps. At any rate it should help us to make an identification.'

'Are you going to do anything about it?' asked Owen. 'When you've found out who it was?'

'Probably not. It's not illegal.'

'I know, but –'

'Yes. I know.'

It was an issue that the Parquet generally fought shy of. Charges of some sort could certainly have been brought but the case would probably have gone to the Native Courts, where it might well have been thrown out. The Native Courts were the most traditional of the courts and unlikely to have any doubts about the practice itself. As for the consequences, while they were undesirable and unfortunate, they were also, one might say, in the natural way of things. The practice was so deeply embedded in social custom that it was, besides, something of a political hot potato. Even the Nationalists steered clear of it.

'It's not illegal,' Mahmoud repeated.

That for him was usually decisive. He had been trained in the French School of Law and had a thoroughly French frame of mind. A thing was either legal or it was not. If it was legal, then it was no concern of lawyers. If it was illegal, then that had to be spelled out.

All the same, Owen could see that he was not happy.

The release of the findings had the desired effect. Public interest in the Maiden disappeared entirely. No one, after all, cared much about a woman dying. Certainly, of natural causes.

The next morning Owen presented himself at the Department of Irrigation. When he learned what Owen wanted, the clerk threw up his hands.

'Effendi,' he said tragically, 'there is only I.'

Owen looked round the office.

'There is not,' he said. 'There are Yussef and Ali and Selim and Abdul. Not to mention the man who has gone out to make the tea.'

'But, Effendi –'

'As well as the people in the next office. And the one after that. And what about –?'

'Effendi, we are as grains of gold in a desert of sand!'

'I'm sure you are. But how about getting on with –'

'Does the Effendi want *all* the names?' asked the clerk despondently.

'Certainly.'

'But surely only of those fine men who are on the permanent strength?'

'I want the names of all those who are working on the barrage at the moment.'

'But, Effendi, they are legion!'

'How legion are they?'

The clerk consulted his ledger.

'At this time of year, Effendi,' he said impressively, 'sixteen thousand.'

'Not working on the barrage at the moment, there aren't. About two hundred, I'd say.'

'But, Effendi, they are for the most part worthless fellows, mere villagers, who come up here for the Inundation, work for a few weeks and then return to the dreadful place from where they came!'

'They are the ones I am particularly interested in. First, I'd like disciplinary cases –'

'But, Effendi, they are *all* unruly, mere savages –'

'Then injuries.'

'But, Effendi, what does it signify if a few are injured? When we think of the general good? If a few fall by the wayside or into the river?'

'And the dismissals.'

'Effendi, at the end of the Inundation they are *all* dismissed, and a good thing too –'

'The ones who are dismissed *before* the end.'

'But, Effendi, why bother about the few whom Macrae Effendi and Ferguson Effendi have shrewdly seen have got it coming and wisely advanced the hour?'

'Just see I get the names tomorrow,' said Owen.

When Owen went into his office the next day, Nikos, his official clerk, had the list in front of him. Owen was taken aback by the remarkable burst of productivity. Then he saw the reason. The list had only five names.

'No dismissals, two injuries, minor, the rest, wages docked for being late,' said Nikos. 'That what you wanted?'

Owen frowned.

'I want to know first if it is true,' he said.

Nikos nodded.

'I'll check,' he said.

'And while you're doing that, can you look a bit more widely?'

'What for?'

'Possible reasons for a grudge. I'm after motive.'

Nikos was looking through the list.

'They're all Corvée men,' he said. 'You can tell by the payroll numbers.'

'They will be at this time of year. It's the height of the Inundation.'

'I was just wondering if that could be anything to do with it.'

The Corvée was the name given to the system by which the Government had traditionally summoned up labour each year to maintain the river banks and watch the dams when the Nile rose. In the past the system had been full of abuses. Virtually every able-bodied man between fifteen and fifty had been called up and obliged to work unpaid for a substantial part of the year away from his own land. Worse, the great Pashas, or noblemen, had frequently contrived to divert them to work on their own estates, flogging them if they refused. Anyone then might well have had a grudge against the system.

But not now. When the British had come they had abolished the Corvée, at least in its old form. Now the work was voluntary, paid, and for a shorter period. And the Pashas' abuses were twenty years in the past. Surely, thought Owen, no one could harbour a grudge for so long? Even in Egypt, where grudges were sometimes nourished for generations.

When Owen entered the Gardens he experienced a mild shock. They were covered with water. For a moment he thought that something must have gone wrong at the regulator and the canal overflowed. But then he realized. This was Thursday and watering day throughout the city.

Every Thursday water was pumped up out of the river and distributed through the city in pipelines to parks and public gardens, where it was drawn off locally into systems of raised earth ditches, called gadwals.

That was what had happened here. The Gardens looked like a vast shallow lake out of which the trees and shrubs jutted incongruously. In the water between them hundreds of birds were playing. Palm doves crouched and crooned. Hoopoes hesitated inhibitedly like bathers on an English beach. Bulbuls and sparrows, not at all inhibited, splashed water over their backs in a furious spray. Brightly-coloured bee-eaters, never still, swerved and dived. Buff-backed herons stalked and stabbed. There were even some green parakeets, released deliberately from Giza Zoo to see if they would breed wild.

Owen hesitated a moment, wondering how to cross the Gardens and get to the regulator dry. Across the water he saw the gardener, up to his ankles and bent over a gadwal, and made a gesture of inquiry. The gardener pointed to a path leading up into the trees. It ran along the slight crest beside the valley he'd walked through previously and took him nearly to the regulator.

At the regulator things were quieter. A solitary cart had been backed up to the breach and from its rear men were lowering sandbags precisely into position with a rope and pulley. Ferguson was lying on his front peering down into the breach and directing proceedings. He stood up when he saw Owen coming.

'We've got something for you,' he said.

He called down to Macrae, who came up and joined them. They walked down the canal to where what looked like a piece of broken pipe had evidently been heaved up out of the water.

'What is it?'

'It's part of the culvert. From just beside the regulator gates. It was blown out by the explosion and carried here by the water. The thing is, though: see those? They're burn marks. That means, that's where the stuff was put. Just shoved up inside, I'd say.'

'Aye,' said Ferguson. 'That would have been enough. It's the position, you see. It would have cracked the concrete that held the frame just by the hinge. The weight of the water would have done the rest. Whoever did it knew just what they were doing.'

'And you still say,' said Owen, 'that it wasn't one of your workmen?'

31

3

The gardener came running.

'Effendi! Oh, Effendi!'

He arrived panting.

'Oh, Effendi! Another one!'

'Another what?'

'A bomb! Oh, Effendi, come quickly!'

'Another! Jesus! Where?'

The gardener pointed across the Gardens.

'The Rosetta? Jesus!'

They ran straight across the Gardens, splashing through the water. Birds scattered. Herons rose with a clap of wings like a gunshot. The palm doves rose in a flock. Hoopoes hesitated no longer and made for the trees.

The gardener ran ahead of them, his bare feet kicking up the water. He led them across the lawns and then up on to the crest along which Owen had passed previously. Down into the bamboo clumps of the valley and then left along the stream, almost to the spot where the ghaffir had been taking his repose. There, virtually beneath the baobab trees, the gardener halted.

'But –?' began Macrae.

'There, Effendi, there!' pointed the gardener with trembling finger.

He was pointing towards a gadwal.

'Leave this to me!' said Macrae, shouldering Owen aside.

'Aye,' said Ferguson. 'We know about these things.'

He pushed Owen behind a tree and then went forward to join Macrae.

'Bloody hell!' they said in unison.

Owen, who had served with the Army in India before coming to Egypt, and thought he also knew about these things, re-emerged from behind the tree and went cautiously up to them.

They were peering into the gadwal. Lying in the bottom were a pair of detonators.

'It is easy to see, Abdullah,' said the ghaffir superciliously, 'that you are not a man who knows about dynamite!'

'How was I to know?' said the gardener defensively. 'It looked like a bomb to me!'

'How did you find it?' asked Owen.

'I was clearing the gadwal,' said the gardener. 'You need to, to make sure that the water can flow along it. You'd be surprised what gets into it. Leaves, sticks, that sort of thing. All these birds! And then the people – they put rubbish in it, though you'd think they knew better. So before I let the water through I go along and see there are no blockages. I mean, you don't want water coming over the sides until you're ready, do you? What would be the point of that? You may not think I know about dynamite,' he said aside to the ghaffir, 'but I do know about gadwals. Mess up one and you've messed up the lot!'

'Gadwals!' sniggered the ghaffir. 'To talk about gadwals when the Effendi have great things on their mind!'

'Never mind that!' said Macrae. He looked down into the gadwal. 'Spares, you reckon?' he said to Ferguson.

'Aye,' said Ferguson. 'Discarded afterwards.'

Macrae picked them up.

'And you know where they come from?' he said.

'Aye,' said Ferguson.

The stores were kept in a hut beside one of the regulators. Its door was heavily padlocked.

'I doubt they went that way,' said Macrae.

He led them round to the back of the hut. The lower part of the rear wall was masked by a profusion of the mauve, thrift-like flowers that grew everywhere in the Gardens.

33

Macrae pulled them away. At the very bottom of the wall a hole large enough for a man had been neatly cut in the wood.

Ferguson went round to the front again and unlocked the padlock and they went in. The hut was full of equipment neatly arranged on racks. There were spades, picks, drilling bits, coils of wire, nails, screws, packs of various kinds. There was a stack of the wooden trug-like baskets that were still universally used along the banks for carrying earth in. There were piles of the traditional wooden shovels.

Macrae went over to one of the walls and pulled aside some stacks. Behind them was a stout wooden chest with huge iron clasps and a padlock even stronger than the one on the door. Macrae unlocked it and looked in.

'Aye,' he said.

'Detonators?' said Owen.

'Four missing.'

'That would be right. And dynamite?'

'At any rate,' said Macrae sourly, 'there's some left.'

'A padlock's no good,' said Ferguson. 'We'll have to find somewhere else to keep it.'

'Have you a storeman?' asked Owen.

'He's all right,' said Macrae. 'I'd trust him with my life.' And then, catching Owen's sceptical look, he added. 'Aye, I know what you're thinking. But he's all right. I've known him for years. He was with me down in Aswan. Got injured in a fall, so I put him in charge of stores. That was six years ago and we've never had cause for complaint.'

'Never!' said Ferguson.

'Does he have keys?'

'No. I open up and lock up each day,' said Ferguson.

'And we're the only ones with keys to the box. We each keep a set in case there's a sudden need and one of us can't be found. But no one else has a key.'

Owen bent and looked at the padlock. It was a fairly standard one. The storeman might be honest but people would be in and out of the hut all day and one of them might well have been able to size the padlock up, even, perhaps, take an impression while the storeman was distracted.

The hole in the wall had been hidden by some sacks.

'Aye,' said Macrae, 'but it can't have been done long before or we'd have found out.'

'The same night?'

'It would take a bit of time to cut,' said Ferguson. 'Maybe the night before.'

They went round and looked at the hole again from the other side. Whoever had cut it had dug himself a shallow burrow in the sand for extra concealment while he worked.

'Yes, but Ibrahim ought to have seen him,' grumbled Macrae. 'He's supposed to look all round.'

He summoned the ghaffir and showed him the burrow.

'What's this, then?'

Ibrahim studied it.

'A lizard, Effendi?'

'Lizard, bollocks!' He indicated the hole. 'This was a man!'

'Yes, Effendi,' said the ghaffir unhappily. 'A lizard man.'

'I can see, Ibrahim,' said the gardener maliciously, 'that you are not a man who knows about thieves breaking in.'

'I know about thieves breaking in,' said the ghaffir indignantly. 'Ordinary thieves, that is. But this was a lizard man. Lizard men are different.'

The phrase unfortunately caught on. Walking past some of Macrae's workmen later, Owen heard them discussing the latest developments, which, of course, by this time they knew all about.

'. . . a lizard man, they say . . .'

'Ah, well, there's not much you can do about that, then, is there?'

'I don't like it. If he's got it in for us, then there'll be trouble!'

The newspapers picked it up. Waiting for Mahmoud that evening, sitting at an outside table in the big café at the top of the Mouski, Owen heard a new cry from the boys selling newspapers.

'Lizard man! Lizard man!'

He bought a newspaper to find out all about it. It was as he feared. Prominent on the front page was the heading

LIZARD MAN STRIKES!

Beneath, was a lurid and totally inaccurate account of the attack on the regulator.

That kind of detail, however, was of little interest to the newspapers, which, at this corner of the Mouski, were largely Nationalist in tone. They preferred to speculate on the Lizard Man's identity. Was he, for a start, a Nationalist? A number of the newspapers seemed to think so. They saw the whole thing as an attack on the British.

LIZARD MAN HERO STRIKES AT BRITISH DAM!

ran one of the headlines.

Other newspapers, however, pointed out that the Regulator was not British but Egyptian. Who would be so dastardly as to attack an Egyptian dam? Clearly, the inspiration was Christian. But not necessarily British. The British, for all their faults – and the newspaper listed a half page of them – were not lizard men. They had no need to be, because they controlled the show anyway. No, it was someone more insidious, someone who preferred to lie low and conceal himself in the sand; the Lizard Man was a Copt!

A Coptic newspaper, not surprisingly, took a different view. The Muslims, relative newcomers in the country (they had arrived a mere twelve hundred years ago), had never really appreciated the great architecture that had preceded them. They had seen it as the work of Satan. Was it surprising, then, that they should strike at one of the great buildings of modern Egypt? The Lizard Man was plainly a Muslim, almost certainly of a fundamentalist persuasion.

Various other newspapers took various other views. They agreed, however, on certain major points. The Lizard Man had done it, and he was aptly named, for he struck surreptitiously and he did reptile things. Like the snake, he snatched the young from the mother's nest and the mother's breast. All women should, therefore, be warned!

The authorities were, naturally, seriously concerned. The Mamur Zapt himself was on the trail. Unfortunately, if reports were correct, he had allowed himself to be led on a wild lizard chase . . .

'What's this I hear about a lizard man?' asked Mahmoud, dropping into the chair opposite Owen.

'A figure of daft speech,' said Owen.

'There are plenty of those around. Myths of Maidenhood, for a start.'

It was, in fact, the Maiden that Mahmoud wanted to talk about, although not in her mythic incarnation. The release of the autopsy's findings had brought him certain leads and he thought he was now close to establishing the Maiden's identity. That was not the problem.

'The problem is that Labiba Latifa has got hold of it.'

'Labiba Latifa?'

'You've not heard of her?'

He had, just. Mahmoud filled him in.

Labiba Latifa was a lady of independent means and independent spirit who in her youth had trained as a nurse – abroad – and on her return occupied herself with a number of good causes, most of them in the field of health. That she had been able to do this so publicly had been in large measure due to the position of her husband, who had been the Dean of Cairo's Medical School. When he had died, she had proposed to carry on in exactly the same way.

That, however, was a quite different thing. While widows, especially wealthy ones, were accorded more leeway in Egyptian society than most women, the prominence of her activities and the outspokenness of her views had soon brought her notoriety. Even in reformist circles, opinions of her were mixed, some feeling that progress was more likely to be made in quieter ways. She was altogether a formidable lady; as Mahmoud had found when she had come to see him.

She said that she had read the findings of the autopsy with interest, and asked him what position he proposed to adopt on the case.

Mahmoud had replied, with strict correctness, that he proposed to adopt no position on the case. His task was simply to present such evidence as he could to the inquest.

Labiba had asked him if that would include evidence that she had died of the effects of circumcision. Mahmoud had reminded her that these were only the preliminary findings; but if the final report was to that effect, then he certainly would.

What verdict did he expect? And what action was likely to follow?

Mahmoud, honest to a fault, replied that he thought it highly unlikely that any action would follow.

Was he satisfied with that?

Mahmoud had replied, truthfully, that he wasn't.

So what did he propose to do about it?

Owen imagined that there must have been quite a silence at this point. Eventually Mahmoud had said that he didn't know.

Labiba had nodded her head.

What did she expect him to do, Mahmoud had asked?

Labiba had said that this was a case in the public eye, and that the right thing to do was to make an issue of it.

Mahmoud had said that this was hardly up to him. His role was to serve the law as it stood. If wider issues were raised by the case, then they would be identified either by the court or by the Parquet.

Was there nothing that he, as investigating lawyer, could do, Labiba had asked? And waited.

Mahmoud was much too sharp not to understand how he was being pressurized, and to recognize that his integrity was being skilfully called into play. Labiba had done her homework and knew her man.

He had replied neutrally that he was still at an early stage of his investigations and if when he had completed them there were issues to be raised he would consider the matter then.

He had braced himself for further pressurizing. Instead,

Labiba had merely nodded her head again, as if accepting what he had said. He had realized afterwards that this was a clever way of binding in his commitment.

She had then, to his surprise, completely switched tactics. In fact, she had confessed, she was not sure herself how to proceed in the circumstances. Could she discuss them with him?

Following the publication of the autopsy findings, the case had been brought to her attention by a group of midwives with whom she had dealings on other matters. They had been especially concerned about the age at which the circumcision had taken place.

'Opinions differ, Mr el Zaki, – even amongst midwives – on whether female circumcision is in itself an acceptable practice. I have my own views on the matter and they are clear-cut, but I do have to recognize that they are not universally shared, especially in the poorer, more traditional quarters. The group of ladies in question live out beyond the Khan-el-Kahlil and they usually disagree with me on such issues. We do not, however, disagree on the fact that if it has to be done at all, it is best done at an early age. In this case, as you know, the poor girl was twenty.'

'Why, then, was it done?' asked Mahmoud.

'She was going to get married. Late, yes, but she was the only woman in the household – her mother died some years ago – and I fancy her father did not want to lose her services about the house. However, the opportunity of a profitable marriage came up and he couldn't afford to miss it. Now, the bridegroom was very much older than she was and very traditional in his thinking. He would certainly expect her to be circumcised. Indeed, the marriage might well have been off if she wasn't. So –'

'Why hadn't she been circumcised before?'

'Her mother had died. These things are usually seen as women's matters and there was no woman to see they were done.'

'No one else in the family?'

'They had moved from the country. The father is a water-carrier, poor, and' – Labiba sniffed – 'very ignorant. Do you know what is the greatest cause of crime in the country, Mr el Zaki? Ignorance. Not even poverty, for we can be poor without being ignorant. Admittedly, the two usually go together.'

Mahmoud bowed his head gravely. He had expected a lecture at some point.

'So he knew no better. That is why, Mr el Zaki, I am in some difficulty. On the one hand the case is in the public eye, and an issue of principle is involved, an issue which we can make narrow enough – the age, not the fact, of circumcision – to enlist public support. On the other, the person in the dock should be ignorance, not some poor, lowly, uneducated man. Nor the poor, lowly, uneducated woman who performed the circumcision.'

'You know the woman?'

'I do.'

'And the girl?'

'I know of her.'

'So,' said Mahmoud, putting down his coffee and looking at Owen, 'the issue of principle is very close.'

Which way Mahmoud would go on the issue when the moment of decision came, Owen did not know. No one could rise as far and as fast in the Parquet as Mahmoud had done without being worldly wise. Yet there was at the same time an odd streak of naiveté in Mahmoud which took the form of an obstinacy about principle. He remained, thought Owen, as he walked down to the river the next morning, an idealist at heart.

He was on his way to see how preparations for the Cut were getting on. As he neared the point where the Khalig Canal came out into the river and where the Cut would be made, there were increasing signs of the coming festivities. Banners had appeared on some of the houses and brightly-coloured strings of bunting hung across the streets.

He had arranged to meet McPhee and when he turned a corner he saw him ahead of him. Along with a group of small boys and half the neighbourhood he was watching the public crier crying the height of the river.

'Fifteen digits today and still rising!' the crier intoned sonorously.

A hand was pushed through the lattice-work of one of the harem windows above and some coins thrown down. The crier scooped them up swiftly before the small boys got to them and bowed to the window.

'Blessed be the mistress of this house!' he called.

'Digits?' asked Owen.

'On the Nilometer,' said McPhee.

It stood at the end of Roda Island, just opposite them.

'It's very important, you know,' said McPhee. 'In the old days it used to relate to tax. There was a law which said that you couldn't levy land-tax until the river had reached a height of sixteen cubits. Very sensible, really, because people's capacity to pay depended on the irrigation of their land. Of course, the Government used to fake it.'

The dam, a simple earth one, ran across the canal just at the point of its entrance into the river opposite Roda Island. Its top was now only some six feet above the level of the water but its builders had been in this business for a thousand years and knew what they were doing.

Some way in front of the dam, in the dry bed of the canal, a tall cone of earth had been constructed. Its top had been sown with millet.

'Obvious fertility associations,' said McPhee.

When the Cut was made, and the dam breached, the water would pour through and demolish the cone, to the great satisfaction of onlookers. In the past, tradition had it, a young virgin had been sacrificed simultaneously, no doubt to their even greater satisfaction.

'Although there is possibly some confusion here,' said McPhee. 'You see, the cone is also called "The Bride" – the Nile, as it were, impregnates it – and popular imagination may have distorted that into a real woman.'

Popular imagination was still alive and kicking in Cairo and one of the distortions it had threatened was the absorption of Mahmoud's dead young woman into the traditional story. That had been stopped, fortunately, by the release of the autopsy findings. There was little purchase for the popular

41

imagination in a woman who had died in so apparently ordinary a way.

McPhee, however, was reluctant to let the connection go.

'You don't think,' he said wistfully, 'that the woman who was found –'

'No,' said Owen firmly, 'I don't.'

He made the mistake, however, of telling Zeinab about it when they met for lunch at her father's house later that morning. It was a mistake firstly because female circumcision was exactly the kind of topic likely to intrigue Nuri Pasha.

'It is a barbaric practice,' he said, 'and I am totally opposed to it. They say it improves the woman's beauty, that unless you do it, the labia minora dangles unbecomingly, but I have never been able to see that myself. I have always felt that the more a woman is developed in that area, the better. And then the cutting pares away the most interesting parts. It diminishes the woman's capacity for pleasure. I am totally against that,' said Nuri, shaking his head. 'It diminishes mine.'

He looked tenderly at the latest painting he had acquired: a Renoir nude. Nuri was fond of things French; especially women.

'It's a lower class practice, of course. But, do you know, my dear, I was talking to Shukri Pasha this week – he's just taken another wife, she's only fourteen, but a beauty, I gather – and he told me that when Khadiya came to him – she is his second wife – or is it his third? – anyway, when she came to him he was astonished to find that she had been circumcised. "My dear Shukri," I said, "that's what you get if you marry out of your class." Anyway –'

He continued happily for some time.

'Anyway, my dear,' he said suddenly to Zeinab, 'that's why I didn't have you circumcised.'

'I'm glad you didn't,' said Zeinab. 'I wouldn't have wanted to miss out on anything.'

Zeinab was the second reason why it was a mistake to raise the subject. She wasn't very interested in circumcision but she was interested in Labiba Latifa. Modern in spirit, although not quite in the way that Mahmoud was, Nuri had raised his daughter to be independent. That was a very difficult position for women to be in in Egypt at that time and Zeinab was eager to hear about others in the same position.

'Do you think she would like some help?' she asked suddenly.

'No,' said Owen.

It was Greek day in the Gardens. There was a festival of some sort and they were doing their national dances. The women were in traditional costumes, in which a fine lawn chemisette seemed to play a great part, and danced in a group, with much spirited skipping and rhythmic stamping of feet. The men were dressed more drably, in shiny black clothes and black wideawake hats. They took off their coats and waistcoats to dance, but were less stripped down than the Levantines, some of whom came in singlets, as for the gymnasium. Their women, too, appeared to be feeling the heat, for they had removed their dresses and were sitting in their petticoats, retaining, however, the white wreaths round their heads.

A pretty young woman danced across to Owen.

'He's in the shade,' she said, 'with the beer.'

She took Owen in among the bamboos to where a rug had been spread for a picnic. There was a hamper but no beer. Rosa, who knew her husband's habits, led Owen further into the shade. Georgiades was standing beside a gadwal talking to the gardener. He was embracing an armful of bottles.

'I was asking him if he could let some water into the gadwal,' he explained.

'And I was telling him I couldn't,' said the gardener. 'This isn't the right day.'

'I was just wondering if you could make an exception,' said Georgiades, fishing in his pocket.

The gardener looked at the coins.

'No,' he said. 'I couldn't. Look, there's a stream just over there. Why don't you put the bottles in that?'

'It's too far.'

'For God's sake,' said Rosa. 'Why don't you dance, like the other men?'

'Yes,' said Owen, eyeing the Greek's bulk. 'Why don't you dance, like the other men?'

'Besides,' said Georgiades, ignoring all these remarks, 'there are always thieves about in a place like this. I'll bet you've had some trouble –'

'Well,' said the gardener, 'as a matter of fact –'

Owen walked back with Rosa to the picnic place.

'I suppose you wouldn't like to dance?'

'I'm not familiar with the Greek dances,' Owen excused himself.

'Perhaps there wouldn't be much point,' Rosa conceded.

She had always had a soft spot for Owen, especially since that business of the ransom. Indeed, if ever Zeinab should fall by the wayside, and if, by any unfortunate chance her husband, too, should be struck down, then – She brushed aside the possibility that Owen might have his own views. Rosa believed that whoever her mate was, she and he would be of one mind; hers.

She offered him some tsatsiki. While he was eating it, she squatted down beside him and asked about the regulator.

'You know,' she said, looking in her husband's direction, 'he's not really the man for this. Water is not a liquid he's had much to do with. And he knows nothing, absolutely nothing, about gardens. I'm the only flower he's heard of.'

'I know,' said Owen, 'but he's a wonderful man at getting people to talk to him.'

Georgiades and the gardener were coming back through the bushes.

'Yes, well, I could put them in the stream, I suppose,' Georgiades was conceding, 'but I'm not happy about it. Not with all these thieves about. Now if there was a ghaffir around –'

'Him?' said the gardener. 'He'd be the first to take them!'

At the regulator all was calm. The water winked placidly in the sun. Some papyrus heads which had crept through the main barrage circled slowly up to the breach and then spun away again. The workmen were sitting up on the bank. Macrae and Ferguson stood on top of the regulator looking down into the breach and conferring.

'We've stopped it up,' said Macrae. 'Now we've got to find a way of letting the water through again.'

'But controlled,' said Ferguson.

'We're thinking of using the undamaged gate. It's the other one that's the problem.'

'Aye,' said Ferguson.

They took Owen back to their little office and produced coffee. Then Macrae sat back.

'We've talked to the men,' he said.

'Talked to the men?'

'Aye. About the dynamite. We've told them it won't do. Now I don't mind the odd spot of pilfering. But dynamite is different.'

'Yes, but –'

'Y'see, that hole in the shed was clean cut. It was done with proper tools. Now we reckon that whoever did it must have brought his tools with him. And there's a chance that the other men might have seen them. Of course, there's also a chance that he brought them some other time and kept them hidden. But they keep close together and there's a possibility that one of the others may have seen something. So we put it to them.'

'Put it to them?'

'Aye. We said now was the time to speak up. This wasn't a private thing, this was a matter for everyone. Everyone suffered from a thing like this and if it happened again they would suffer more, their own villages, their own people.'

'And what did they say?'

'They didn't say anything. But they will.'

'They've got to talk it over first, you see,' Ferguson explained.

'And you think it will work?'

'Aye,' said Macrae.

4

In the Gardens the dancing was continuing furiously. The women had formed into a long line, their hands on the hips of the one in front of them, and were snaking about all over the place. The men had dropped back into a stationary row and were clapping the rhythm. The women danced up to them teasingly and then withdrew. Owen could see Rosa about half way down the line, plainly enjoying herself.

The dancers' families had turned out in support. He recognized Rosa's parents and formidable grandmother surrounded by lots of little children, themselves dressed for dancing, who must be cousins. Rosa belonged to a large extended family and to marry her was to marry the whole Greek community. Georgiades, a communal backslider, had had little choice in the matter. The marriage had been arranged; by Rosa.

Georgiades himself was nowhere to be seen. Owen began to walk round the group to greet Rosa's family but then spotted him, beyond the dancers, among the bougainvillea, sitting on the edge of a gadwal talking to the ghaffir.

'Lizard men!' he was saying in appalled tones as Owen came up. 'I wouldn't meddle with them if I were you!'

'Don't worry!' said the ghaffir fervently. 'I won't!'

Owen stepped back behind a bush.

'Mind you,' said Georgiades, 'it could already be too late.'

'Too late!'

'Yes. I mean, you saw him, didn't you?'

'No! All I saw was his trail. I mean, I knew at once that it was a lizard man, you can tell by the marks, it's their tail. But that's not the same thing. I didn't actually see him, not him himself –'

'Well, then, you were a lucky man!'

'I know, I know!'

'I mean, you could so easily have seen him. It must have taken him some time to make that hole –'

'Ah, no, it wasn't like that. I mean, they don't work like that. Not lizard men.'

'They don't?'

'No. They don't do it themselves, they get men to do it for them. That's why you don't see them. And that's the way it was here. The wood wasn't gnawed, was it? It was cut. If a lizard man had done it himself, it would have been gnawed. You don't see lizard men with tools, do you?'

'Well, no –'

'No. He got someone to do it for him. Someone who had the tools. Then he came along afterwards, wriggled through the hole, took what he wanted and then was on his way.'

'Well. I still think you were lucky. Because you could so easily have seen him at that point, couldn't you?'

'Yes, but I try to take care. I mean, that's always the risk in a job like mine. You've got to be careful you don't see too much. If you just go blundering around, you can easily walk into something, and then, bang! The next minute you're in trouble.'

'So what do you do?'

'I creep. Then if you come across something, if you see something, or, more likely, hear something, like that night –'

'So you *did* see him?'

'No, no. like I said, you don't see them. They get someone to do it for them.'

'Ah, so *that* was the one you saw?'

'I didn't see anyone. But –' the ghaffir lowered his voice – 'I knew he'd been there.'

'Well, the hole, of course –'

'No, no, not that.'

'How, then?'

The ghaffir laid his finger along his nose.

'Fair is fair, and if you take mine, I take yours. That's fair all round, isn't it?'

'Depends what it is,' said Georgiades.

But the ghaffir seemed to think he'd said enough. He picked up his gun and prepared to move away.

'All the same, though,' he said, with a slightly worried expression on his face, 'it's best not to meddle with the Lizard Man.'

Mahmoud seemed oddly uneasy. Normally, although he was on the best of terms with Owen personally, he liked to keep his distance from him over legal matters. Constitutionally there was no place for the Mamur Zapt in the legal scheme of things, and Mahmoud was a stickler for constitutionality. Over this business of the Maiden, however, he seemed anxious to consult him at every turn. Owen knew that it was not because he had any doubts over the right course to pursue in terms of law. It must be something else; and Owen thought he knew what that was.

Mahmoud was not at home with this kind of case. It touched on things he knew very little about: women, for example. By this time most Egyptian men of his age would have married. Mahmoud's father, himself a busy lawyer, had died young, however, and before he had had time to arrange that. Mahmoud had had to set about supporting his family and had immersed himself first in his studies and then in his career to the exclusion of all else. His mother broached the issue from time to time, indeed, was doing so with increasing frequency, but Mahmoud, determinedly modern, made it clear that he himself would see to the matter when the time came.

The time, however, had not so far come; and, since he had no sisters, and was, like many educated young Egyptians, distinctly prudish on sexual matters, the consequence was that he had had very little to do with women and knew very little about them. Given the way in which women were kept from any contact with men outside their own family, Owen doubted whether Mahmoud had ever spoken to a young woman of his own social standing.

The result was, thought Owen, that Mahmoud probably knew as much about female circumcision as he, Owen, did about water engineering.

And it was from this weak basis that Mahmoud was being called on to make a major, probably public, stand. Had the law been clear, Mahmoud would not have hesitated a moment. But the law, wisely, in Owen's view, had left the matter vague. This was, as things stood, as much an issue of morality and social policy as it was of law.

Again, had things been clear, Mahmoud might well not have hesitated. He was, as Labiba Latifa had found out, a man of strong moral principle and firm social convictions. But he did like things to be clear, he needed them to be clear. And were they clear here? Mahmoud simply did not know enough about the subject to know whether they were or not.

And so he was unusually hesitant, unusually uncertain.

'I was wondering,' he said diffidently, 'if you would like to come?'

'By all means.'

They set out down the Mouski, on foot, because at this time of the evening the street was so full of people that even if you took an arabeah from one of the hotels, whose drivers were the most aggressive in Cairo, it wouldn't have been able to force its way along at more than walking pace. Up near the Ataba the shops were quite good but the nearer one got to the bazaars, the cheaper and shoddier they became and the street was virtually taken over by stalls.

They forced their way through the crowds around the nougat sellers and Arab sugar sellers and – Owen could never quite understand this – spectacles sellers and made their way into the Khan-el-Khalil, the Turkish Bazaar. It was the bazaar most popular with tourists, who were there in throngs, studying the saucers of glittering gems, the lumps of turquoise, the flashing and densely-chased silver- and brass-ware and the gaudy keepsakes of Crusaders and Pharaohs. The shopkeepers were all in black frock-coats and tarbooshes. It was Oriental, all right. But not Egyptian.

Behind the bazaar was the real Egyptian: small, poor houses with the doors open and people sitting in them, catching the air; small, poor, dimly-lit shops with black-clad women fingering the last remaining – and reduced – tomatoes; stalls again, this time with sticks of sugar cane, small cucumbers and pickles.

It was here that Um Fattouha, Mother Fattouha, lived. She was one of the midwives in Labiba Latifa's circle of contacts and the one, Labiba thought, most likely to be of use to Mahmoud.

Mahmoud stopped at the open door and called softly in. A large, fat lady, heavily veiled and dressed in black, came to the door. She led them into an inner room. It was very dark, lit by a single spluttering oil lamp, and furnished only with a single worn divan and a floor cushion on which a young man in the dark suit of an office worker was sitting, nervously playing with his tarboosh.

He sprang up when they entered.

'Suleiman Hannam,' he introduced himself. 'Labiba Latifa told me to come. I – I knew Leila.'

The woman indicated that they should sit on the divan and then disappeared. The young man returned to the cushion at their feet.

'How did you know Leila?' asked Mahmoud.

The young man swallowed.

'I – I had known her before,' he said, 'when we were children. Back at our village. Then her family moved away. I had forgotten about them but then one day I saw her father, in the street. I was wondering whether to go up and speak to him when I saw her. She was bringing him his lunch. I guessed at once that it was her. But she was so different! So – so –'

'So?'

'Womanly. I just stood there. All I wanted to do was look at her. She went away, but I guessed that she did it every day, so the next day I found out where he would be and I – well, I went there, and waited for her. And then I followed her home.'

'Did you speak to her?'

'No. Not at first. I just wanted to see and I followed her every day. And then one day she – she realized. At first it frightened her and just made her hurry all the more. But then – then she saw how it was. And then one day – one day she smiled at me –'

Owen sighed inwardly.

Mahmoud, however, frowned. This was loose behaviour.

'Smiled?' he said. 'Was she not in her veil?'

'Oh yes. But I – I knew somehow.'

Mahmoud looked stern.

'And then?'

'Well, I – one day I approached her. Not that day. Much later. I – I went up to her. And spoke.'

'You spoke to her without asking her father's permission?'

'He wouldn't have given it me. Our families – our families had quarrelled. Years before. In the village.'

'You shouldn't have spoken to her.'

'I meant no harm! I – I spoke to her honourably.'

'How could you speak to her honourably? Without her father knowing, and your father knowing?'

'I was going to. I wanted to. Only – only Leila said I should wait. And I thought, perhaps that was a good idea, perhaps I would be able to talk my father round –'

'Wouldn't that have been better?'

'It would have been difficult. The daughter of a water-carrier! He would have been very angry.'

'All the same –'

'I would have tried. We agreed that was best. Only –'

'Only what?'

'One day she told me her father was going to marry her to Omar Fayoum.'

'Well –'

'But he's old! And foul! And not really very rich. All he does is run a water-cart. Well, that may look good to a water-carrier but it's nothing really. I thought I would go to him and say, look, you can do better than that. I have a job at the Water Board, and if you will only wait – But Leila said no, the fates were against us, and I said, let us defy fate –'

Owen groaned again; inaudibly, he hoped.

Mahmoud, however, became fierce.

'Did you touch her?' he demanded.

'No! I would never show her any disrespect, never –'

'Are you sure?'

'Never! Never! I was honourable, she was honourable. She was always honourable. She –'

The boy dissolved in tears.

'All right, all right. All right!'

'Never!' sobbed the boy.

'All right! So what did you do?'

'Do?' The boy looked at him in surprise. 'We didn't do anything.'

'You must have done something. What happened next?'

'Nothing. Leila said we must stop seeing each other now that she was betrothed.'

'So –?'

'So we stopped seeing each other.'

'Come on, you don't expect me to believe that!'

'Just the once. I said I had to see her, she owed it to me. And then –'

'Yes?'

'I pleaded with her. I pleaded with her for hours. But she said no, she was betrothed, it was different now, and we must stop seeing each other.'

'And what about the next time?'

'There was no next time.'

'You just went away?'

'No. Not at first. I – I hung around. But she wouldn't see me. And in the end – yes, I went away. The fates were against us!'

'And you never saw her again?'

'Never. I wanted to, but – Then one day I heard.'

'That –?'

'That she was dead.'

'How did you hear?'

'My work brings me down in these parts sometimes. I went into a shop to buy some oranges and I heard the women talking.'

'And then you went away again?'

'What else was there to do?' the boy said.

After the boy had gone, they talked to the woman.

No, she said, she hadn't done it, although she knew who

had. It had all been very difficult because there was no mother to act on Leila's behalf. If there had been, all this wouldn't have happened. Leila would have been circumcised years before.

'But that fool of a father –'

The mother had died soon after they arrived in Cairo and the father had not married again.

'That was a mistake; the girl needed a mother.'

They were, of course, desperately poor. The father had been a simple water-carrier. It was one of the humblest jobs in the city. All you needed was a water-skin. Then you would go down to the river, fill it and then walk through the streets offering it for a millieme or two to the thirsty.

From a very early age Leila had had to take on the duties of the woman in the house, cleaning, cooking, carrying – even the water had to be fetched. From an early age, too, each day she had taken her father's lunch to him.

'Too much for him to carry, I suppose,' said Um Fattouha tartly. 'Though you'd have thought he'd have got used to carrying.'

With no woman in the house, Leila had been almost indispensable to him.

'That's why he wouldn't let her marry. It's not that there weren't inquiries. There's plenty of mothers who wouldn't mind their son marrying someone who worked hard and didn't complain.'

But of course he had known that he would have to let her go at some time. You could always get a woman in to do the housework. A marriageable woman, though, was worth something more than just her labour. The trouble was that she was a depreciating asset and the longer you left it, the less she would fetch.

'So when old Fayoum came along, he had to do some hard thinking. Well, it wasn't that hard. Fayoum was worth a bit – well, to a water-carrier, anyway. There was a chance, too, they say, of a job on the cart itself, and when you're getting old, that's the kind of job you fancy. So he didn't have to think too long.'

It was only when they began to think about the wedding –

and there were plenty of women in the street who were ready to help him think about the wedding – that the problem was spotted.

It arose when they began to think about the wedding night itself and were making arrangements for the depilation.

'Old Fayoum's not going to like that,' they said. 'He'll think there's something wrong.'

So they went to see Leila's father.

'That's all right,' he said. 'There's still plenty of time. Just get on with it.'

It was here, though, that opinions had begun to diverge, for some of the women hadn't liked it.

'She's too old,' they said. 'Since it's got to this stage, it's best left as it is.'

But Leila's father had been adamant.

'Now it had got so far, he didn't want anything to go wrong. He was counting on that job on the cart, you see.'

A number of the women who had been approached had been unwilling to do it. Um Fattouha herself had refused.

'I might have done it better than that old bitch,' she said, 'but even if it had gone right, there would still have been problems, wouldn't there? At her age it would have taken time to heal. Just think of the wedding night if she wasn't ready!'

In the end, though, someone had been found and the operation performed.

'Well, it went wrong from the start. There was that much blood! Or so I hear.'

Leila had never recovered. She had lingered on for a few days and then died.

'And that old bastard was too mean even to bury her properly!' said Um Fattouha indignantly. 'He just threw her into the Canal like a bit of old rubbish!'

The swollen river lay uneasily within its banks. Even in the last day or two it had risen noticeably. Now as you walked along the embankment the water was lapping at your feet. The launch came right in to the bank. Owen hardly needed to step down. Along the banks the women were doing their washing, their silver anklets flashing in the sun. Further along, the buffaloes were lying in the water like hippopotami. The great stretch of the barrage rose up ahead of them.

Ferguson was waiting at the landing stage.

'Aye,' he said, 'it's full. And when it's full, it's never still. It's straining, you see, straining to break out. And when it presses, it finds all the weak spots.'

They walked through the Gardens to the engineers' office, built out of the same sun-baked clay as the houses of the workmen further down the canal. In the early days they had built it of wood but then had found that wood was much hotter than clay, particularly when the walls were thick and the windows small.

Macrae was sitting at a table bent over a drawing. Overhead a fan was whirring. He looked up and pushed the drawing away.

'So you've come,' he said.

'I came as soon as I got your message,' said Owen.

'Aye,' said Macrae. He seemed unenthusiastic; even cast down.

'We'd better have some coffee,' he said. 'This is a bad one.'

He went to the door and called. A boy, who had clearly been waiting, promptly appeared with a tray. He set it down on the table with a beam of white teeth

Neither Ferguson nor Macrae were beaming.

'Well,' said Macrae abruptly, 'you were right. It was one of our own.'

Ferguson shook his head.

'We told you we'd put it to them about the tools. "Someone must have had tools," we said. "And if anyone brought a tool kit in with them one day, the chances are that one of you would have seen it. Now, we're all in this together – it's like the village back at home – and if you saw it, you must tell us. Otherwise it could happen again!" Well, that's what we said, and then we left them with it. They like to talk these things over, you see, among themselves. One of them would never come to us on his own. They're all part of the group, and it's what the group decides. We just left it to them and, well, this morning they came back to us.'

'With a name?'

'Aye. Babikr.'

'I'd never have thought it of him!' said Ferguson.

'It just shows how you can be deceived in people,' said Macrae.

'Aye.'

They drank their coffee dispiritedly.

'He's always been quiet!'

'I thought he just liked to get on with it.'

'Well, he *does* like to get on with it. We've never had any complaints, have we?'

Ferguson shook his head.

'Babikr!' he said bitterly.

'They gave you his name?' said Owen.

'Aye.'

'Does he know? That they've given his name?'

'Must do.'

'Then he'll be off unless we – Where is he?'

'They'll be down by the regulator.'

The men were taking their morning break. They were sitting up on the bank, unusually quiet.

There was no need to ask about Babikr. He was sitting apart from the others, his knees drawn up to his chin, arms round them, head bowed.

Owen went up to him.

'Babikr,' he said, 'you must come with me.'

'You know why I have taken you?'

'Yes, Effendi.'

'You broke into the store?'

'Yes, Effendi.'

'And took the dynamite?'

'Yes, Effendi.'

'And what did you do with it?'

'I put it beside the gate. In the culvert.'

'And detonated it?'

Babikr nodded his head wordlessly.

'Why, Babikr?'

Babikr shook his head.

'Was it because of something Macrae Effendi had done to you?'

'No, no, Effendi –'

'Or Ferguson Effendi?'

'No, Effendi,' said Babikr, distressed.

'Someone else, perhaps? Here at the barrage?'

The man shook his head.

'Or in the Department?'

Again the shake.

'Why then, Babikr?'

He waited a while and then repeated the question. The man did not reply.

'No one does a thing like this without reason,' said Owen. 'What was your reason?'

Babikr just tightened his lips.

'Perhaps something bad had been done to you?'

Babikr shook his head firmly.

'No, Effendi. It was not that.'

'Then what was it?'

'The Effendis have always been good to me.'

'Someone else?'

'No one else.'

Owen sat back bewildered.

'Is it that you are angry against the Khedive?'

'The Khedive?'

It was almost as if the man had never heard of him.

'Or the British, perhaps? Come, man, you may say it.' Owen smiled. 'There are plenty who are.'

Babikr shook his head.

'You are not –?' Owen wondered how to put it. With a more educated man he might have said 'a Nationalist'. Or if uneducated, in Cairo he might have asked whether he was a member of one of the 'clubs'. Or even of one of the gangs. But this man was a simple fellah, up, for a while, from the country.

'You are not, perhaps, a follower of Mustapha Kamil?'

Mustapha Kamil had been for a time the charismatic leader of the Nationalist movement. He was now dead but many nationalistically-minded Egyptians still identified with him.

At least they would have heard of him. Babikr, however, clearly had not.

'But why did you do it, Babikr? Surely you can say?'

Babikr, however, could, or would, not. In the end, Owen shrugged and let it rest. The man had confessed. That was all that was needed.

It would be helpful, though, to have some corroborative evidence. He asked the man about breaking into the stores. On this he was quite prepared to talk. Yes, he had come in one night and cut the hole. He described it so circumstantially as to put it beyond doubt that he had done it. Vague, as all fellahin, about dates, he was not able to specify the day. It had not been the same day as he had blown up the regulator. It would have been too much for one day.

He had hidden the dynamite for a night or two in a disused gadwal before taking it to the regulator and using it.

And his tool-kit?

Here Babikr needed no encouragement to talk. It had been stolen.

Stolen?

Yes, that very night. In the Gardens. While he was taking the dynamite to its hiding-place. It had been too much to carry both it and the tool-kit so he had hidden the tool-kit temporarily, intending to come back for it. When he had done so, he had been unable to find it. He had come back again the following morning, thinking he had just made a mistake about the place, and had looked for it thoroughly. In the end he had been forced to realize that somebody had taken it.

'While I was there, Effendi, in the Gardens. In the Gardens! I tell you, Effendi, there are thieves everywhere!'

There were, indeed, and Owen had a pretty good idea of one of them. He sent for the ghaffir.

The ghaffir denied it vehemently.

'Would I do a thing like that, Effendi?'

'Almost certainly.'

The ghaffir still denied it. Owen had his house searched. A small saw was found which Babikr identified as his. He asked after the rest of the tools. After some prevarication the ghaffir admitted he had sold them. Owen sent men to recover them.

The ghaffir changed tack.

He had done it, he said, only to punish the intruder.

'You can leave punishment to me,' said Owen, and detailed the consequences that would follow if he had any more trouble from the ghaffir.

'So,' said Owen, 'you were watching all the time?'

Not all the time, said the ghaffir. The workman had already started when he got there. As he was coming through the trees, quietly, he had heard suspicious noises.

'Then, Effendi, I crept. I feared there might be many, and I, but one. So I went forward with circumspection. And, lo, there was a man crouched at the back of the hut.'

'Crouched? Not lying down? I thought he had made a burrow?'

'No, no, that was the Lizard Man. He came later.'

'Did you see him?'

'No, no, Effendi. That would have been very unwise.'

'But you did see a man crouching?'

'Yes, Effendi. And I lay there and watched him. And after a while he stopped working and crawled through into the store to see that all was well for the Lizard Man. Then he came out and gathered his tools and took them and hid them in a gadwal. And then he went off into the trees.'

'Carrying something?'

'I could not see, Effendi. The night was dark. And I thought, I shall play a trick on him. To punish him. Yes, that's right. To punish him. So I stole forward and found the tools and took them away with me. Ho, ho, I thought, that will teach you a lesson!'

'Fair is fair,' said Owen, 'and if you take mine, I take yours. Is that it?'

The ghaffir looked at him, surprised.

'Well, yes, Effendi. That was it, more or less.'

'And you did not think to seize the man?'

'Well, no, Effendi. He was bigger than I.'

'Were you not armed?'

'Ah, yes, Effendi. But so might he be.'

'Nor did you think of reporting it the next morning?'

'By then, Effendi, it was surely water under the bridge.'

'And, besides, you had the tools?'

'Well –'

'And thought, no doubt, that was punishment enough?'

'Exactly so, Effendi,' agreed the ghaffir, relieved.

Owen had one last question.

'You know the workmen; and you saw the man. Which of them was it?'

After some hum-ing and haw-ing, the ghaffir identified Babikr.

'Well, that clinches it,' said Macrae.

'Aye,' said Ferguson despondently.

'Ye'd never have thought it.'

'One of ours!'

'I still can't understand it. Why would he do a thing like that?'

'You think you know them,' said Ferguson, shaking his head.

'Well, you do know them,' said Owen. 'You reckoned that if you put it to them, they'd come out with it. And you were right.'

'Aye. There is that.'

'Still, one of ours –!'

'What I can't understand,' said Macrae, 'is how he could bring himself to do it. You've met our men,' he appealed to Owen, 'you can see what sort of men they are. Now, would they do a thing like that?'

'Well –'

'No more would he. At least, that's what I would have said.'

'Someone must have got at him,' said Ferguson.

'Aye. That's what I'm thinking. And do you know what more I'm thinking? I'm thinking that it's not over yet. If they can turn one good man, they can turn another. They might try it again. I shan't feel happy till I know what's behind this.' He looked at Owen. 'I hope you weren't thinking of stopping?'

5

McPhee stuck his head in at the door.

'I'm worried, Owen.'

'You are? About what, particularly?'

'The licentiousness.'

'Licentiousness?'

Owen put his pencil down.

'I don't know that we can do a lot about that, can we?' he said cautiously.

McPhee came further into the room.

'I do feel that we ought to make some effort to, well, *contain* it.'

'I'm not sure –'

'You see, Owen, there will be mothers there. And children. Not to mention the Kadi.'

'Ah, you're talking about the Cut?'

'I am sure it must make him uncomfortable.'

'I don't know. He's been opening it for centuries, hasn't he? I would have thought he was pretty used to it by now.'

'And then there's the Diplomatic Corps.'

'Licentiousness? That's hardly likely to trouble them!'

'And think of the Consul-General's wife!'

'She's not involved, surely?'

'No, no. But she will see it. That's the point. It's pretty unavoidable. I do feel people ought to be protected against immodesty, Owen.'

'Well, I . . . You don't think she could just stay away? If it bothered her?'

'But, Owen, she goes every year!'

'Well, then . . . Surely, that means –?'

'Owen!' said McPhee severely. 'She goes out of a sense of duty!'

'I'm sure, I'm sure. Only –'

'Yes?'

'I don't see what I can do about it.'

'Couldn't you ban some of the more outrageous forms of behaviour?'

'Such as?'

'I really wouldn't like to specify,' said McPhee, cheeks growing pink.

'That makes it difficult.'

'I just feel,' said McPhee earnestly, 'that something ought to be done. Before it is Too Late.'

'McPhee thinks I ought to ban immodest behaviour,' said Owen, as he and the Consul-General's Aide were leaning on the bar of the Sporting Club that lunchtime.

'Certainly. I'll speak to the Diplomatic Corps about it.'

'No, no. He means in general.'

'Isn't that the Kadi's business? Religion, morals and all that?'

'But he's going to be opening the ceremony!'

'Well, then, doesn't that suggest that he thinks it all right? I mean, his view of what constitutes immodesty might be different from that of a Scottish Presbyterian.'

'I think I shall go to the Cut this year,' announced Zeinab.

'McPhee is worried about the immodesty of the proceedings.'

'Then I shall certainly be going,' said Zeinab.

Yussef, Owen's orderly, put the mug down and waited.

'Yes?'

'Effendi, the whole office will be going.'

'Going? Where?'

'To the Cut.'

'All right, you can go.'

'Thank you, Effendi. It is not for me I ask, but for my wife.'

'You are taking her? Well, that's very nice.'

'Yes, Effendi. She believes it will make her fertile, you see.'

'Really?'

A thought struck Owen.

'Just a minute. I thought she was fertile? Haven't I been giving you days off –? Let me see, how many of them? Five, six, seven –'

'But that's it, Effendi! It works, you see!'

All Cairo seemed to be quickening at the prospect of the festivities. More and more bunting was appearing in the streets around the canal. Along the river bank, boats were breaking out in flags. Enclosures for spectators, carpeted (on the enclosing fences, not the ground) were rising at both ends of the dam. Anxious overseers came twice a day to inspect the earthworks.

'Fifteen and a half digits!' cried the crier.

Gardeners were perpetually watering the maize on top of the 'Bride of the Nile' and patting the cone into shape. The other Maiden, found beneath its base, seemed, fortunately, to have been forgotten.

There had been a telephone call for him in his absence.

'From a woman,' said Nikos.

This was remarkable. The telephone system in Cairo was still in its infancy and mostly confined to Government offices and businesses, in neither of which did women figure largely; indeed, at all.

'You're sure?'

'Of course I'm sure!' snapped Nikos testily.

The reason for the testiness was apparent when he revealed whom the call was from: Labiba Latifa. Nikos was not used to women; still less was he used to female steamrollers.

Owen rang her back.

'Ah, the Mamur Zapt! So pleased!' she said. 'I understand you're taking an interest in this poor girl?'

'No,' said Owen hastily. 'No. Absolutely not!'

'That's strange,' she said. 'I understood that you were.' She hesitated. 'But surely,' she said, 'you were with Mahmoud el Zaki when –?'

'Coincidentally. Yes, coincidentally.'

'A fortunate coincidence, though. For if it were known that the Mamur Zapt was taking an interest –'

'I'm afraid not. Not formally, that is. I am afraid that as Government officers we have to keep to our remits. And mine is the political.'

'But this *is* political.'

'Not in my sense of the word. Which is rather strictly defined.'

'The trouble is,' said Labiba, 'that there is a danger of the case falling between stools. Stools which are over-strictly defined. I suspect that Mr el Zaki feels much as you do.'

'That is the problem,' said Owen, 'when you talk to Government officers. Perhaps you should really be talking to politicians?'

'I always find it difficult to bring things home to them. Whereas when a Parquet lawyer is assigned a case, it is hard for him to deny that it is something to do with him.'

'I am sure that Mr el Zaki will do everything he can. Unfortunately, I, myself –'

'I understand that you were involved because of the connection with the Cut?'

'I don't think there is any connection. There was a risk at one time of one being wrongly made because of where the body was found but I think that risk has now diminished.'

'Actually,' said Labiba, 'that is what I am ringing about.'

'Oh?'

'I think the risk has grown again.'

'Of course, there will always be ill-informed people who talk –'

'Not entirely ill-informed; the girl's father.'

He asked Mahmoud if he could go with him. It was Mahmoud's case; but if there was any possibility of those stupid – and potentially troublesome – rumours about the Maiden reviving he meant to get in there and kill it off quick.

The man lived out beyond the bazaars, on the very edge of the old Arab city, just where it gave on to the Muslim graveyard and the desert. The streets in this part of the city were full of crumbling and decaying houses, many of them still beautiful. Beyond them, though, were houses which were not beautiful, little squat blocks, single-storey and single-room, made of cheap sun-baked bricks which the rain, sometimes hard in Cairo in winter, was already dissolving. The walls had shrunk and the roofs sagged, so that some of the buildings were now only half the height they had been, and you had to crouch to go in and crouch while you were inside. Many of them were shared, as in the countryside, with animals. But these were the richer houses.

Out here on the very rim of the city, all semblance of street plan had been lost. There were gaps everywhere and great stretches of rubble, which the sand, drifting in from the desert, was slowly covering. They stopped uncertainly.

Some men were digging in the graveyard. Mahmoud asked them if they knew the house of Ali Khedri. One of the men nodded and then, glad of the excuse, put down his spade and came out to accompany them.

'The house of the water-carrier,' he said, pointing.

It was one of the poorer houses. The walls had caved in so badly that the doorway had almost disappeared. You had to drop on to hands and knees to go in.

Inside, everything was filthy. There were some rags in a corner, some water-skins thrown down carelessly, and over by the rear door some pots and pans. They did the cooking outside, presumably.

'It needs a woman's hand,' said the water-carrier defensively.

He was a short stocky man dressed not in the usual galabeeyah but just in woollen drawers. His skin had been burnt black by years of working in the fields and then walking in the streets. His eyes were reddish and inflamed, the usual ophthalmia of the fellah in the Delta.

'We lived better than this once,' he said. 'I wanted to give it her again.'

'Through marriage to Omar Fayoum?'

'Well, why not? I know they said he was too old for her. That's not the point, I said. It's not how old you are, it's how rich you are. And you don't usually get rich until you get

65

old. It takes time. That's my experience, anyway. There are advantages, too. All you've got to do is hang on and one day he'll be gone. And then you'll have it all. That's what I said. That's what I said to her, too. Oh, I know he's not young and handsome. I know he's a hard old bastard. But that's not it. The point is, he's got a piastre or two. He's got one cart, he's talking of getting another. That's real, that is. It's not just a pair of nice brown eyes.'

He spat on the floor.

'Brown eyes!' he said contemptuously. 'They're not real.'

Ants were already gathering around the spit. There must be something in it, thought Owen. Sugar? Tobacco? Hashish?

There was another stain just beside it. From it a moving column stretched across the floor and up the wall. Not ants, not cockroaches, either; some other sort of bug.

'It needs a woman's hand. I've never said she wasn't good about the house.'

'And yet you were going to marry her off?'

'She was getting on. It would soon have been too late. I hung on as long as I could. And then old Omar comes along. "It's now or never," he said. "In another year she'll be over the hill." Mind you, I think he'd had his eye on her for some time. He was just waiting for the price to drop. "You don't want them young and skittish," I said. "Not in a wife, anyway. You want them hard-working and strong." "I like them a bit skittish," he said, with a grin. But he was ready to take her, all the same.'

'But first he wanted her circumcised?'

'No, no. He didn't know anything about that. He took it for granted that she was. I took it for granted that she was. Her mother ought to have seen to that. Back at the village. It was only when they were putting the sugar paste on that they found out. Then they came to me fast. She's not right, they said. Well, then, you'd better make her right, I said. And it was then we got into all this stuff about her being too old and him being too old.'

'But you went ahead with it?'

'Well, it would have been off, otherwise, wouldn't it? Omar Fayoum is not going to want anything that's not a hundred per cent, is he?'

And now Owen's ankles were itching. There were almost certainly fleas. They were all three squatting on the floor. There was nowhere else to sit.

'So it was done?'

'Yes.'

'And then it went wrong?'

'That old bitch! I don't reckon she knew what she was doing when she did it. And I paid her good money, too! Not all, luckily. Some before, some after. When it came to after, I went to her and said: "You old bitch, you've done it wrong. I don't mind paying good money for a good job, but this isn't a good job, is it?" So I docked her some. Well, then she set up a great crying and shouting. It wasn't her fault, she said. She said it was because the girl was too old. But she didn't say that before, when we were making the deal! "You've cost me money," I said. "Now she's fit for nothing. She might not even be fit for old Omar when the time comes."'

'She was very sick?'

'Couldn't lift a finger. Just lay there. "This won't do," I said after a while. "You've got to pull yourself together, my girl."'

'You didn't call a hakim?'

'Hakims are for rich people. When you're poor, you've got to get better by yourself.'

'All the same –'

'Besides,' said Ali Khedri, 'by that time it was too late.'

'Too late? Why?'

'Because I'd thrown her out.'

'Thrown her out?' said Mahmoud incredulously.

'Yes. I didn't have much choice, did I? Not when I found out.'

'Found out? What did you find out?'

'About her and this boy. To think that all the time I'd been arranging things with Omar Fayoum, she'd been carrying on with that little bastard! "I love him," she said. "Love?" I said. "What's that? How much is that worth? How much does that fetch in the market, then? And how much do spoiled goods fetch? You tell me that! You've brought shame and dishonour upon me," I said.

'Oh, then she wept and said it had amounted to nothing and it had all come to an end anyway and that she would marry Omar Fayoum if I wished.

'"Wished?" I said. "What's that got to do with it? Do you think he's going to have you now? Or anyone else is, for that matter? You've made your bed, my girl, and now you've got to lie on it. Only you're not going to lie on it in my house. Not in the house that you've brought disgrace upon!"

'Well, then she wept and clung to me and begged me to let her stay. She'd work, she said, and find some way of bringing in some money. "I know your sort of work," I said, "and if you think I'm letting my daughter go out whoring, then you'd better think again, my girl. I may be poor but I'm not that poor. Out on the streets is where you belong and that's where you'd better go!"'

'So she went?' said Mahmoud, tight-lipped and angry.

'Yes.'

'And you made no attempt to find out what had happened to her?'

'I wasn't going to ask. I thought that maybe she and that boy – But I kept seeing him around, he was always creeping around, and someone told me he was forever asking about her, so I reckoned that couldn't be it. Then I thought that maybe someone would tell me, but no one did. And then one day I heard about that woman at the Cut, you know, that woman they found buried under The Bride. Well, at first I thought nothing of it, but then –'

'Yes?'

'Well, I know some of the gravediggers, you see. And one of them has a brother who works at the mortuary. And he told him that he reckoned the girl that was found was my Leila. How he could tell, I don't know. From what the man said who'd found her. But it set me wondering. And what I asked myself was, how did she get there? There, of all places? Well, someone must have put her there, mustn't they? And they must have done it for a purpose. And do you know what I reckon?'

He looked at Owen and Mahmoud almost triumphantly.

'It was the Jews.'

'Jews!'

'Yes. They go in for this sort of thing, don't they? And then there's the Cut.'

'What has the Cut got to do with it?' demanded Owen.

'It's the last one, isn't it? That makes it a bit special. Well, what I reckon is that they wanted to mark it out, this being the last one, and it being their turn. They take it in turns, you see, them and the gravediggers from the cemetery here. I don't know that I hold with that, really, but it's been like that for centuries, they say. Turn and turn about. Well, this time it was their turn and I reckon they wanted to mark it out, this being the last time.'

'What are you saying?'

'Well, that they put her there. It was the old tradition, you see. Bury a virgin under The Bride. And I reckon they thought that would round it off nicely. They're great ones for tradition, the Jews. It was probably them who thought of the idea in the first place. Only I don't hold with that, not with putting a good Muslim girl under the cone. Now if it was a Jewish girl, that might be different –'

'You think they found your daughter and buried her under The Bride of the Nile?'

'Not found her.'

'Not . . . ?'

'Killed her. The bastards.'

'She died,' said Mahmoud, 'from the effects of poorly performed circumcision. And from neglect and ill treatment afterwards. If anyone killed her, it was you.'

They walked back up the Suk-en-Nahassin past some of the most ancient and beautiful mosques in the world, past the Sultan-en-Nasir, the Sultan Kalaun and El-Hakim, past the fountain house of Abd-er-Rahman and the Sheikh's house next to the Barkukiya. The past was all about you in Cairo, thought Owen. That was the trouble.

By tacit mutual consent they dropped into a café just before they got to the Khan-el-Khalil. Both were feeling depressed.

'What do I do?' said Owen. 'Put him inside until the Cut is over?'

'The Cut is not the problem,' said Mahmoud.

'No,' agreed Owen sadly.

Back in the office he said to Nikos:

'There's an old man down by the Muslim graveyard. Ali Khedri. A water-carrier. He's probably harmless but I don't want him saying things that could cause trouble.'

'You want him picked up?'

'No. But I want someone down there keeping an eye on things. Until the Cut is over.'

'Georgiades?'

'No. I want him to stay in the gardens. He'll like that.'

'What's he supposed to be doing there?'

'Talking to the workmen. I want him to find out about Babikr. Where he comes from, where he stays when he's up here. Who he talks to. Who – more important – talks to him.'

Owen had been invited to a reception at the hospital. The invitation had come from Cairns-Grant, the pathologist, a man with whom Owen had often had dealings and for whom he had a great deal of respect. When he arrived, the reception was in full swing and Cairns-Grant was talking to fellow-countrymen: Macrae and Ferguson.

'We were talking about the regulator,' said Ferguson.

'And I was asking who could do a thing like that,' said Macrae.

'And I was saying I could,' said Cairns-Grant.

'You could?' said Owen.

'Aye. Half our problems come from the barrages.'

'That's not fair!' protested Macrae.

'What's the commonest disease in the country?'

'Malaria.'

'Ophthalmia,' said Owen.

'Bilharzia,' said Cairns-Grant. 'If you add in ankylostoma, which you should, eighty-five per cent of the male population have it. Why? Because they work in the fields – and because of the irrigation system.'

'I don't see –'

'There's a wee snail. It's a water snail and it's host to the

70

bilharzia parasite. Bilharzia is a water-borne disease. So, for that matter, in this country, are ophthalmia and malaria.'

'But you can't blame it all on the Irrigation Department!' cried Macrae. 'They must always have been here!'

'Aye, but until recently it was confined to the northern parts of the Delta. Now you find it everywhere, all through Middle and Upper Egypt. And why? Because of the irrigation system.'

'Now, come, Alec –' began Macrae.

'It's the change of system, from basin irrigation to perennial, which you get with the barrages. In the old days they would draw the water off into basins and let it lie there until it soaked away, leaving the silt. After that they left the land alone, which gave the sun a chance to cauterize it – I'm talking medically, ye understand – killing off the shell fish left behind by the flood.'

'But the basin system was very inefficient, Alec. You could only get one watering and therefore one crop a year, now you can have watering all the time and therefore two or sometimes even three crops. You've got to think of the cotton, Alec. It's increased production no end.'

'Aye, but it's also increased bilharzia, that's what I'm saying. Eighty-five per cent of the population, man! It leaves them anaemic and debilitated. There's been an actual decline in the health of the population over the past forty years. And it's getting worse. So,' said Cairns-Grant, 'if I was one of the young Nationalists, instead of throwing a bomb at the Khedive or the Consul-General, or maybe, more sensibly, the Mamur Zapt, I would throw one at the barrage!'

'Well,' said Macrae, taking his arm, 'I hope no one's listening to you.'

Across the lawn a middle-aged lady, Egyptian, was advancing on them.

'My favourite lassie!' cried Cairns-Grant, delightedly. 'Have ye met?' he said to Owen. 'Her husband was Dean of the Medical School here. Labiba Latifa!'

'We were speaking only this morning,' said Labiba, shaking hands.

'You were? Well, you don't need me to tell you then, Owen, that she's a formidable lady. You see that?' He pointed to a long, low building beside the hospital. 'It's the Midwifery Extension. And it wouldn't have been there if it hadn't been for her!'

'Oh, come, Alec!' she said.

Owen guessed that she seldom addressed people, even at parties, without purpose; guessed, too, that he was her purpose.

'I have to thank you,' he said.

'You have spoken to him?'

'This morning.'

'And what are you going to do?'

'I don't know.'

'Sometimes it is right to hesitate,' said Labiba, as if she was talking of a novel experience.

'In my position you always have to think of wider consequences,' said Owen.

'Is that a reason for action or for inaction?' asked Labiba.

Owen smiled.

'In your case, for action, I am sure. My interest, though, is often in prevention.'

'Perhaps our interests are not always dissimilar,' said Labiba. 'I have come to ask you for a favour, Captain Owen.'

'I will do what I can,' said Owen, 'although –'

Labiba smiled.

'I shall come back to you later on – well, on the more general issue. My favour, this time, is a particular one. It concerns Suleiman Hannam.'

'That young boy? The one with –?'

'Yes, the one you met at Um Fattouha's. I would like you to speak with him. I am afraid he may do something foolish.'

'What in particular?'

'He is very confused. I think it is because it is the first time he has met death. He cannot accept it. He knows, of course, in his heart of hearts, that nothing can bring Leila back. But he believes – half of him believes – that if in some way good could come from her death, that would probably redeem it, give it and her life a meaning which at the moment it seems to lack. That is why he came to me.'

'Because of your work on circumcision?'

'Yes.'

'I am afraid I still don't see – Do you wish me to dissuade him?'

72

'Hardly! The reverse, if anything. The activity would do him good!' Labiba brightened. 'Yes,' she said gleefully, 'that would be good. To have the Mamur Zapt proselytizing on my behalf! They would really think I was formidable then! But, no, Captain Owen, that was not what I wanted you to talk to him about. It is the other half of him. The other half of him is angry. It is looking for someone to blame.'

'To take revenge on?'

'Well,' said Labiba, 'is that not our Egyptian way?'

Macrae caught him as he passed.

'We're having a wee celebration,' he said. 'Tuesday, the Sporting Club, at eight. Burns Night. Would you like to come?'

'Nothing I'd like more!' Then a thought struck him. 'But surely Burns Night isn't for some time yet?'

'Aye. But it goes down better if you have a few rehearsals.'

Zeinab, stretched out beside Owen, had been hearing about his encounter with the girl's father.

'It is a good job my father is rich,' she said sombrely. 'And enlightened. Relatively.'

Zeinab always liked to hear about the women in his cases. She tended to identify with them strongly. It was as if, uncertain of her own position in society, she needed to try on other positions. It always made him feel guilty. He was aware that what would give her position was marriage. But the British Administration did not look kindly on its officers marrying Egyptians. And what about her father's attitude? Nuri, he knew, would have preferred her to marry someone rich. That was the way, he thought, with fathers; perhaps not just in this society.

What made the difference, though, between Zeinab and Leila was that Zeinab did not have to do just what her father said. Perhaps, however, that was an illusion. Perhaps in the end she did have to do what he said, perhaps there were limits to her freedom. Meanwhile, though, there was the space created by wealth, which allowed indulgence. And, to be fair, by enlightenment. Relative, that was.

'I gather you're going to talk to the boy.'

'Yes.'

Wait a minute: 'gather'?

'You've been talking to Labiba!'

'Certainly. She is a remarkable woman.'

That, no doubt, was another role that Zeinab had been try-ing on. Widow. Widow! Surely there were better solutions than that!

Nikos looked up from his desk.

'A call for you. Urgent. From the Parquet.'

'Mahmoud?'

'Someone in his office. Would you meet him at the Mortuary?'

Again the slow journey by arabeah.

'One has to think of the horse, Effendi. And of the people in the way. And of the flowers in the gardens and the doves in the trees.'

'I'll think about them. You think about getting me to the Mortuary.'

In fact, they made speedy progress. At this hour in the after-noon, when the world was taking its siesta, the streets were empty. Search as the arabeah driver might for reason for delay, he could find none. Even the horse, made brisker by a little breeze from the river, and finding motion cooler than standing stunned in the sun outside the Bab-el-Khalk, quickened its usual step.

Mahmoud was waiting for Owen at the door of the Mortuary, standing in its cool shadow. He was holding a piece of paper.

'It's an early warning,' he said.

'Warning?'

'That they're going to change the autopsy findings.'

'On what grounds?'

'Cause of death.'

'Not –?'

'– what we thought. They've found a ligature around her neck. A thin cord very deeply embedded. They missed it the first time because of the condition of the body.'

'So –'

'She was garotted,' said Mahmoud.

74

6

'Garotted!' screamed the newspapers.

The news, despite Owen's efforts, had leaked out at once. Ordinarily it would have created no stir. In Cairo people were being garotted all the time, or it felt as if they were, and what was one among so many, particularly if she was merely a water-carrier's daughter? This time, however, there was something different.

'Could there be a connection with the Cut?' asked the newspapers.

'No, there could not,' said Owen, and to make sure he excised the suggestion from the newspapers. Censorship of the press was one of Owen's barmier duties.

The press, always resourceful, came back the next day, less directly.

'Will this cast a blight over the forthcoming festivities?' it enquired.

'No, it won't,' said the Mamur Zapt, and in the interests of conviviality he cut that out, too. He knew, however, that in the circulation of rumour word of newspaper was less important than word of mouth, and sat back resignedly to await developments.

They were not long in coming. There was trouble with the Muslim gravediggers, said Paul over the phone. When Owen got to the meeting, however, he found that the trouble, at first sight, was not what he expected.

'There seems to be some problem about the Cut,' said Paul, who had convened the meeting on behalf of the Consul-General.

'It's about who does the actual cutting,' said Garvin.

'I thought we'd settled that. Isn't it the Jews' turn?'

'Yes, but if you remember, there was the problem about the pay. They wanted extra because it was the Sabbath.'

'Well, we've fixed that, haven't we? I got the Old Man to speak to Finance.'

'Yes, but now the Muslims are saying, why should the Jews be paid extra? It's rank discrimination. There's a traditional rate for the job. Why should they be paid more?'

'Because they won't do it, otherwise.'

'Ah, but the Muslims say *they* will. At the old rate.'

'What do the Jews say?'

'They say it's their turn.'

'Has this happened before?' asked Paul.

'It happens every year. There's always been trouble about who was going to do the Cut. The way we resolved it is that they take turns. It's worked up till now. It's just that this year it's different because it's the Jews' turn and the Cut falls on a Sabbath.'

'Couldn't the Jews still do it but at the old rate?'

'They say that the Government would be going back on its word.'

'Well, that's not unknown, is it?'

'They're not going to like it,' warned Garvin.

'The Muslims are not going to like it either,' said the Kadi. 'They're counting on getting the work now.'

There was a little silence.

'How about them both doing it?' suggested Paul. 'Together?'

'They'd be at each other's throats. And don't forget they'd have spades and picks.'

A further silence.

'Why don't we get somebody else altogether?'

'What about the Copts?' said the Copts' representative eagerly.

'There'd be a bloody massacre,' said Garvin shortly.

'I was thinking of British soldiers,' said Paul.

'There'd be a bloody massacre,' said Owen.

Yet further silence. Prolonged.

'We could call the whole thing off. I suppose,' said Paul. 'After all, we don't really need a cut, do we? We don't even need water in the Canal. In fact, it would be better without it. Then they could get straight on with filling it in. Why don't we just call the whole thing off.'

'That way we really would have a riot!'

The meeting adjourned without reaching a conclusion.

'There's still time,' said Paul.

'Not much,' said Garvin. 'The Cut is next week.'

'I do think we should try to resolve this as quickly as possible,' said the Kadi. 'We wouldn't want it to get out of hand.'

'Why should it get out of hand?'

The Kadi looked at Owen.

'I understand something has come up about the girl? You know, the one found under the "Bride of the Nile".'

'The autopsy findings have been revised.'

'Yes. That's what I heard.'

'That Maiden thing? A lot of bosh!' declared Garvin.

'Muslim girl? Jewish diggers? A public occasion? Bad feeling? Big crowds? I don't regard that as a lot of bosh.'

'I don't either,' said Owen. 'I've got people down in the Bab-el-Foutouh keeping an eye on things.'

'If what I have heard is true,' said the Kadi, 'I think I would be down there keeping an eye on things myself!'

At almost any hour of the day near the Bab-el-Foutouh, because of its position next to the Muslim cemetery, you would see a funeral procession coming down the street. First, you would hear the death chant and then into view would come a little procession headed by religious banners and closed by a horned coffin covered with a pall of brocade, borne high on the shoulders of the mourners, who surrounded it and took their turn in the work of merit. Sometimes there would be a bread camel carrying loaves for distribution to the poor and sometimes students of El Azhar carrying a Koran upon a cushion, or fikees reciting.

When such a procession passed, the onlookers would first stand aside respectfully and then press forward behind it in sympathetic support.

This time the procession was a small one and generating interest rather than excitement. Owen stepped in beside a vegetable stall to let it pass.

'It won't be like this when our Leila comes along,' said one of the women shopping at the stall.

'No. She'll get more attention in her death than she ever did in her life,' said another woman beside her.

'It's bad, though. She was a pretty little thing. And to think of her wasting herself on that old skinflint, Omar Fayoum!'

'Ah, well, it didn't come to that, did it?'

'Perhaps it would have been better if it had!'

'She was unlucky, that girl. Her mother ought to have seen to it before.'

'She wasn't there, though, was she? There wasn't any family, either. There was just that mean old man and all he cared about was her bringing him his meals on time.'

'Yes, but you'd have thought someone would have said. One of the neighbours, perhaps.'

'They didn't know. Not till they came to remove the hair.'

'You'd have expected, though, that someone would have taken an interest in her when the mother died. With her being so very young. I mean, what happened when she started having her monthlies?'

'She had to work it out for herself, I suppose. She wouldn't have had any help from that old man, that's for sure. Those water-carriers are a hard lot. Though they do say that when her father threw her out, Fatima took her in.'

'Well, that was something. To think of that poor girl without even a roof over her head! In that condition, too!'

'My old man says that Ali Khedri ought to be sewn up in one of his own water-skins and sent for a sail down the river!'

'So he should! His own daughter! Mind you, she was wrong, too. Carrying on with that boy. When she was going to marry Omar Fayoum.'

'Who wouldn't carry on, if they were going to marry Omar Fayoum!'

Both women laughed, then tut-tutted to themselves reprovingly.

'We shouldn't talk like this, should we? Not about the dead.'

They completed their purchases.

'I wondered where she'd got to. When I didn't see her, I thought she might have gone back to her village.'

'That's where she should have stayed. Why did they have to leave? Water-carrying is no life for a man.'

'She'd have been better off down there, that's for certain. There'd have been women there who'd have known what to do. I've got no time for that old man but really you can't blame him. This is women's business. If she'd stayed down there all this might never have happened.'

'Yes.' They paid and began to move away. 'Mind you –' the woman hesitated. 'They say it wasn't that, you know. Not in the end.'

'What was it, then?'

The woman put her mouth close to her companion's ear.

'They say it was the Jews.'

'The Jews? What would they want with her?'

'What would any man want with a woman? Besides –'

Owen did not quite catch what she said but he saw the other woman stare.

'The Cut? Oh, that's awful –!'

They moved finally away.

Owen found a café in the Bab-el-Foutouh. Save for one thing, you could have gone past it without knowing it was one, since all it amounted to was an open door going down into darkness. Along the front, though, was an old stone bench, at one end of which some men were sitting.

He sat down at the other end and mopped his face. At this season in Cairo the slightest movement made you pour with sweat.

A water-carrier was passing on the other side of the street. One of the men hailed him.

'It'll be a bit easier next week, Abdul, when there's water in the canal!'

'It'll be a bit easier for everyone else too,' said the water-carrier. 'They'll be able to get it for themselves.'

He came across to them.

'From your point of view, then, I suppose it's a good thing they're going to fill it in?'

'Until the pipes get here,' said the water-carrier.

'Pipes? What pipes?'

'They have these pipes which send water all over the city.'

'Well, I'm damned.'

'Or will do. They're doing it quarter by quarter. This one, thank God, is going to be one of the last.'

'But it won't be like the canal, though, will it? I mean, with the canal, all you've got to do is dip your pot in. You can't dip into a pipe, now, can you?'

'They'll have spouts.'

'But then it will all pour away, won't it?'

'No, there'll be taps. You'll be able to turn it on and off.'

'Yes, but still – I just don't see pipes getting anywhere. It'll cost them money to put pipes in. Who's going to pay?'

'You are. They'll charge you for the water.'

'Charge for the water!'

'Yes. And a bit more than I do!'

'God preserve us!'

Owen beckoned the water-carrier over. He gave Owen a little brass cup, undid the top of his skin, bent suddenly forward and shot the water over his shoulder in a glittering jet, straight into the cup.

Owen thanked him and gave him a couple of milliemes.

'No hurry,' said the water-carrier, and stood patiently by while Owen drank.

'Straight from the river?' He took a sip. 'Ah, it won't taste like this when it comes from the canal!'

'It never tastes the same,' agreed the water-carrier.

'It will this time,' said one of the men. 'The Jews are going to freshen it up!'

'With a Muslim girl,' said the water-carrier.

The Muslim cemetery was not walled, although occasional piles of stones indicated its limits, but part of the open desert. The wind blew sand among the tombs, to such an extent that some of the older ones were nearly covered. Only the tops of the tarkeebahs, the stone or brick blocks above the vaults, were visible.

The rich were buried in brick tombs with arched vaults, high enough for the persons inside to sit up comfortably when visited by the two examining angels, Nakir and Neheer. The entrance was at the foot, below ground, so that after the body had been put inside, the earth could be filled in and the entrance concealed. It was not just the Pharaohs who had to bother about robbers.

The gravediggers had just finished constructing the small porch in front of the door of a new tomb, roofed to prevent the earth falling in. Owen joined them in admiring their handiwork.

'It's not bad, you see,' they said, inviting him to inspect. 'The stones fit quite well, considering.'

'Except there,' said one of the men, pointing to a corner. 'That stone was a pig!'

'It doesn't lie flat enough.'

'Why don't you go and get another, then, Hamid, if you're not happy?'

'Because that would make me even less happy.' He looked round. 'It's hard work today. I could do with a drink. Where's that idle sod of a water-carrier?'

'He'll be along.'

'Why don't we go and wait for him, then?'

The men went over to lie in the shade. Owen went with them.

'You need a drink on a day like this,' he said.

'Too true; and out here in the desert there's not much chance of getting one.'

'You'd do better by the river.'

'We don't get much chance of working there. The grave-yards are all this side of the city.'

'You're probably glad when it's your turn to do the Cut, then.'

'We certainly are!'

'I don't see why we shouldn't do it every year,' said one of the men. 'Why do we have to share it with the Jews? What have they got to do with it?'

'It's always been like this,' said another of the men. 'One year it's us, the next year it's them.'

'Yes. But why does it have to be like that, I'm asking? Why shouldn't we do it every time?'

'Because they've got their fingers in the pie and they're not going to take them out.'

'They'll have to take them out after this. Because after that there's going to be no pie!'

'I don't hold with that, either. Why do they have to fill the canal in? It's doing all right as it is.'

'Ah, yes. But that's progress. That's the modern world for you, Mohammed.'

'Well, I could do without it. They're taking everything away from us. Last year it was the Hoseini celebrations, this year it's the canal. Next year we won't even have the Cut!'

'Yes, and it would have been our turn!'

'I like the Cut,' said one of the men.

'Well, yes, so do I. There's something good about seeing a rush of water. Especially when you're used to working out here.'

'Do you think that girl would have made any difference?' asked someone speculatively.

'The one the Jews put under the mound?'

'Yes.'

'Well, I reckon it might.'

'Because I don't see it. I mean, you've got all these bodies up here, haven't you? Why don't they make it all fertile? I mean, if a girl could do it, why can't they?'

'Because there isn't any water. That's just the point. Up here, see, it's all dry and when the bodies get put away, they don't rot. They just sort of mummify. Whereas down in the Canal, when that water comes in, it makes the body rot. Then it's all fertile. I mean, that's the point.'

'So it's a good thing?'

'Well, it's perhaps a good thing to put a girl there. But I don't hold with it being a Muslim girl. Why can't it be a Jewish girl? Or a Copt?'

'The Jews picked her, didn't they? And they wouldn't have picked one of their own.'

'Well, I don't like it. They seem to be having everything their way. First, they get to do the cutting. Then they get paid extra for it! And then they pick a girl who's not even theirs!'

'It's a sort of sacrifice, isn't it?'

'Yes, well, if it's a sacrifice, that means you ought to be giving something up, doesn't it? I mean, if we did it, we'd be giving up one of our girls, wouldn't we? And we wouldn't be too happy about that, because we're advanced, like. But those Jews, they're really crafty. They offer up the girl and say, "here's the sacrifice, let's have something back on account," and all the time they're not offering up one of their own but one of ours!'

'Yes, but God will see through that, won't he?'

'I reckon he already has. The body was found, wasn't it? Well, I reckon that's his way of saying: "No thanks, you crafty buggers, that won't do for me!"'

'Well, I do think he ought not to let them get away with it.'

'Yes, but he needs a bit of help, doesn't he?'

'What do you mean, Abdul?'

'Well, they're going to turn up to do the Cut, aren't they? In spite of everything they've done. And I think somebody ought to teach them a lesson!'

Owen heard the clinking as he turned down a street away from the graveyard and, sure enough, there, coming down the road towards him was a water-carrier. The clinking came from two brass saucers which he was striking together like cymbals to give notice of his presence. Not all the water-carriers had saucers which were brass. Some had mere earthenware ones. Those a step or two up had cups.

Seeing Owen looking at him, the man stopped in the shade. Owen accepted a saucerful, drinking directly from the saucer. Like so many before him. He had learned to stifle qualms.

'The water is fresh,' he said, with the obligatory compliment.

'And heavy,' said the water-carrier.

It was a different man from either the one he had met outside the café or from Ali Khedri. Evidently there were a lot of water-carriers down here, although that was to be expected in so poor a quarter.

'There are some who wait for you with eagerness,' said Owen, pointing to the graveyard.

'The diggers? Well, digging is thirsty work.'

'And carrying. The river is far. Are you not eager for the Cut? The Canal is closer.'

'I like the river,' said the man. 'It is not so far, not when you are used to it. And I like to walk into it with the bags, which you can't do with the Canal.'

'You are a true water-carrier,' said Owen, complimenting him.

'But one of the last. My son will not follow in my footsteps.'

'Because of the pipes?'

The man shrugged.

'Because of everything. This is the last Cut. Next year there will be no canal. The world changes.'

'But the river stays the same.'

'They try to change that. Even in my lifetime I have seen new barrages at Aswan and Assiut and Asna.'

'True.'

Owen handed the saucer back.

'Do you know the house of Fatima?' he asked.

'Ahmed Uthman's wife?'

'I know only that she is the wife of a water-carrier.'

'That would be her.'

The man gave him directions.

'I know one other thing about her,' said Owen. 'She took in the daughter of Ali Khedri when he threw her out.'

The man looked pained.

'That was a bad business,' he said.

'It was well that someone took her in.'

'Not well enough,' said the man grimly.

'How came it that she died when she was under their roof?'

'The Jews took her.'

'Ah? And how do they know it was them?'

'Who else could it have been? With the Cut coming up. But what I know is this: they will not go unpunished.'

'By God?' said Owen. 'Or by man?'

'God, certainly. But sometimes he uses man.'

'What man?'

But the water-carrier could tell him nothing, probably knew nothing, specific. It was significant, though, that the assumption was widespread in that quarter. With the Cut coming up.

'Well, I couldn't leave her,' said the woman, 'not the way she was.'

'It would have been better if you had,' said her husband.

Owen had caught them at the end of the siesta, when the man was just on the point of setting out again. The half-full water-skins lay by the door.

The woman turned on her husband.

'He might have changed his mind,' she said.

'He thought right the first time,' muttered the man, then lapsed into surly silence.

'It was only for a day or two,' said the woman, 'and she eats no more than a bird.'

The house was, perhaps, not as poor as Ali Khedri's, but poor enough. The number of mouths was important in such places.

'How long was she with you?' asked Owen.

'No more than five days.'

'And then?'

'Well, then she went out one day and –' the woman looked bewildered – 'and then we didn't see her any more.'

'The Jews got her,' said the man.

'She went out?' said Owen. 'What for?'

'To meet up with that boy,' said the man.

'No, she didn't!' said the woman angrily. 'She went out to see if she could find any leavings of onions at the stalls.'

'That's what she said,' retorted the man.

'And that's where she was going. She'd stopped seeing that boy.'

'That's what she said!'

'That girl,' said the woman, eyes flashing, 'is as honest as an

Imam. Which is more than could be said of you. And of Ali Khedri, for that matter!'

'Enough, woman!' said her husband, sheepishly.

'And she didn't come back?' said Owen.

'No. After a time I went out to look for her – I thought she might have fallen, you know, she wasn't right yet, not after all that cutting – but I couldn't find her. So I thought –'

'What did you think?'

'I thought, may I be forgiven, that she was with that boy. But then when she didn't come home, I know she couldn't have been.'

Her husband started to mutter something. The woman faced him down.

'When it got on to night,' continued the woman. 'I knew that something must have happened to her. Because otherwise,' she said, looking fiercely at her husband, 'she would have come home. She wasn't that kind of girl. Her heart was pure.'

'If it was so pure,' asked the man, 'how did she get to be talking to him in the first place?'

'Talking is nothing. It's what all women do. It never got to anything more than that.'

'But she didn't come back?'

'No. I went to the *souk*. I asked round the neighbours. I went to the hospital – I thought that maybe she'd collapsed. You know, after all that bleeding. I even,' said the woman, with an edge to her voice, 'went to Ali Khedri.'

'More fool you,' said her husband.

'I walked all over the quarter. I knew something must have happened to her.'

'The Jews got her,' said the man.

Owen turned to him.

'How do you know that?'

'It's obvious, isn't it?'

'No.'

'Well, it's where they found her. Under the Bride. That's not accident, is it? She was put there for a purpose.'

'She could have been put there by anyone. Anyone could have had that purpose. Muslims, Copts. Anyone.'

'Ah, yes,' said the man, unconvinced, 'but the Jews . . .'

'Did she ever have anything to do with Jews? Was she ever seen with Jews?' demanded Owen.

'Well, no. But then she wouldn't have been, would she? They're too cunning for that.'

'But then –'

It was useless, however, trying to talk to him. He couldn't see it. It had to be the Jews.

'They're always creeping around,' he said. 'They're worse than that boy.'

It was the same story as everywhere else.

Coming back through the *souk* he met Mahmoud. He was talking to one of the stall-holders.

'No,' the stall-holder was saying, 'I don't remember seeing her. I wouldn't remember her anyway. She was that quiet! Like a mouse.'

'You remember, though, that she used to come to the *souk*?'

'Oh, yes. Before her – well, you know, before it happened – she used to come most days. Always the same time, just when the stalls were closing. You can pick up a few things then, you know – I mean, if they're going off, you might just as well give them away as throw them away. And the water-carriers' wives – well, they're not too well off. And God says, look after the poor, doesn't he? And it's well to have one or two things to your credit when the Angels come asking their questions.'

'So she would probably have come late?'

'Yes. We don't close till dark. And then we close pretty smartly because if you're not careful those thieving boys will have half your stuff before you can get it away!'

'So she would have been walking home in the dark?'

'She would. And if I could get my hands on –'

The news was already round the *souk*. People talked about it in shocked whispers. In one way it made Mahmoud's task easier, for he had no need to recall Leila to their minds.

He, too, had discovered that when Leila had been thrown out by her father, Fatima had taken her in. He had been checking her story and, although it had all happened some time ago now, had been able to confirm much of it. Neighbours remembered her being 'in a state', as they put it, that night about 'little Leila'. Some of them had, in fact, gone out with her to help in the search. The hospital, surprisingly, had a record of her making enquiries; and Ali Khedri's neighbours confirmed that Fatima had indeed called on him, recalling with relish the altercation that had followed on her rebuff.

The local police themselves could help. Leila's disappearance had not been formally reported to them, but then, in that poor quarter it wouldn't have been. One of the local constables, however, recalled being asked about her. Had a body been found? Several, but none of them Leila's. When, weeks later, a female corpse had been found buried beneath the 'Bride of the Nile', he had wondered if it might be that of the missing girl and had mentioned the possibility to a friend, a gravedigger, who had in turn mentioned it to his brother, who worked at the mortuary. And so it was that long before identification had been officially made, everyone had known all about it. Which was, said Mahmoud, pretty well the usual course of things.

He had been trying to retrace her footsteps that night, without, so far, much success. Even as they were talking, however, one of his men came over and said that he had found a woman who claimed to remember seeing her on the night she disappeared.

'It stuck in my mind,' she said, 'because it was so unusual. And then what with her disappearing – I couldn't help wondering.'

'What did you see?'

'Well, she was talking to someone. A man. Well, she hardly ever talked to anyone, never mind a man! I was that surprised!'

'Did you see who it was?'

'Well, no. It was getting dark, you see, and I just caught a glimpse of them, just as they turned the corner. And I thought: "That's never Leila!" But I think it was, you know, she's such a slight little thing, and she wasn't walking too well, you know, not after –'

She wasn't able to add much more.

'Why didn't you tell someone else?' demanded Mahmoud sternly.

'I did tell someone!' protested the woman. 'I told my husband. But he said: "You stay out of this!" So what could I do?'

'I'll check the husband later,' said Mahmoud, pleased, as he and Owen walked back together, 'but I think we'll find she's speaking the truth.'

Owen nodded.

'It makes a difference. Up till now I've been thinking that the chances were that this was, well, you know, the usual kind of attack. But now –'

'It looks as if she knew him,' said Owen.

'Exactly!' Mahmoud looked at his watch. 'In which case,' he said, 'it makes my next meeting even more interesting.'

'Oh, yes,' said the boy, 'I was down there quite a lot.'

'I thought you said you weren't seeing her,' said Mahmoud accusingly.

'I wasn't. It's my job.'

'You work down there?'

'Sometimes. I'm an inspector with the Water Board. We've got some pipes out that way. I was looking for leaks. Still am, for that matter.'

'In the Gamaliya.'

'We're not out that far yet. In the Quartier Rosetti.'

'Was that how you came to see her in the first place?'

'Yes. And why I was able to go on seeing her. I work on my own and have a lot of freedom. I put the hours in,' he said anxiously, 'but I can take time off during the day if I want to.'

'So you were able to meet her?'

'Yes.'

'More or less when you wanted?'

'At lunch, mostly. When she was on her way to her father to take him lunch. Or on the way back. Not at other times. She was very strict.'

'Did you ever see her in the evening?'

'No.'

'Or at the end of the afternoon? Just, say, when it was getting dark?'

'I don't think so.'

'But you were in the area?'

'Not, really, after dark. I need to be able to see. We've been looking for holes in the pipes. There's been quite a water loss.'

'I'd like to ask you about one specific date: the 27th of June.'

Suleiman took out a diary.

'Yes,' he said,' I was over there that day.'

'Evening?'

'All I've got down is that I had to be over there that day. I wouldn't have thought so.'

'Did you see Leila?'

'No. It was after she'd said – well, that we couldn't see each other any more. In fact – 'he looked at his diary again, 'that must have been about the time that –'

'Yes.'

He put the diary away.

'I didn't know they were going to do that to her. It happened after – after we'd said goodbye. I didn't know till later.'

'How did you find out?'

'I asked someone. When I hadn't seen her for some time, I thought she might be already married.'

'I thought you said that you didn't see her?'

'I wouldn't have spoken to her. I just wanted to see her. And then when I didn't see her, I – I became desperate. There was an old woman, the wife of another carrier, who I knew quite liked her, so – so I asked her.'

'What did you ask her?'

'Where Leila was. I hadn't seen her. And then she told me. She said that women usually had it done when they were younger – that Leila had really been too old – and that it had gone wrong. I can't understand it,' said the boy, 'that they should do these things!'

'Did she tell you where Leila was?'

'Back with her father. I wanted to go and see her. I wanted to go and see him, and tell him – But she said no, no, I mustn't, it would make it worse for Leila, that it was all over and done with now and that there was nothing I could do. I mustn't see her, she said. So, well, I didn't. But I hated him for it. For all he had done to Leila, for marrying her to Omar Fayoum, and then – then this!'

He looked at them passionately.

'These old people,' he said, 'the terrible things they do! They are what is wrong with Egypt. They are killing Egypt. Just as they killed Leila.'

'Killed her?'

'It wouldn't have happened if they hadn't insisted. She was too old for it. And it was wrong anyway. I have spoken to Labiba Latifa and she says it is wrong even for young girls. It is backward, these old people are backward, backward!'

'You hate them,' said Mahmoud. 'Did you hate her?'

Suleiman stared at him.

'Hate who?'

'Leila.'

'How could you think that?' cried Suleiman. 'Leila was all that is good. It is these old people that I hate, her father –'

'She did what her father wished. She would not come with you. She ordered you away. Did that not make you hate her?'

'No, no! Never! I could never hate Leila! She –'

He threw his head down on his arms and burst into tears.

Mahmoud watched him impassively.

Suddenly the boy started up.

'Why do you ask me these things? Why do you say these things?'

'Because the old people did not kill Leila. Someone else did.'

'What do you mean?' Suleiman whispered. 'Someone else did?'

'She did not die because of the circumcision. She died because someone put a cord round her neck.'

'No,' whispered Suleiman, 'no!'

The blood drained from his face.

'They throttled her and buried her in the Canal.'

'No!'

'On the evening of June the 27th!'

'No,' said Suleiman, 'no!'

7

'What is this?' said Labiba Latifa.

'The girl was throttled,' said Owen.

'And Suleiman is suspected?'

'I wouldn't go so far as to say that. Mahmoud will be looking at date, time, place and motive, and will be checking a number of people against these. Suleiman is one of them.'

'Why?'

'Motive, primarily.'

'But surely in Suleiman's case that points the other way? What possible motive could Suleiman have for killing the girl he loved?'

'Love is complex. He might have felt jealous.'

'Of Omar Fayoum?'

'Yes. Or angry.'

'He certainly felt angry. But not at Leila. At about everyone else, I think: her father, Omar Fayoum, the women who had caused her to be circumcised. At everyone old. Suleiman is not a stupid boy, Captain Owen. He could see that it was not Leila's fault, that it was all part of the pattern that women in this country are subjected to. He was angry at the pattern, Captain Owen, not at Leila.'

'No doubt; but Mahmoud has to check all possibilities.'

'Perhaps I can help? You mentioned dates. What dates had Mahmoud in mind?'

'The 27th of June.'

'I will just look in my diary. Time?'

'I cannot say precisely. An hour either side of six o'clock.'

'Then I can help. He was with me.'

'I am sure Mahmoud will be interested to know that.'

'I can be precise,' said Labiba, who was never anything other than precise, 'because I remember the occasion well. It was just after Suleiman had first come to me. I wanted him to see that the issue was not just his alone but something wider, so I took him to a meeting of the Assembly.'

'The National Assembly?'

'Yes. I wanted him to meet Hussein Maktar and a few other people. Mohammed Jubbara, Ali Hamad el Sid, Al-Faqih Mas'udi – You know them, perhaps?'

Owen did. They were all Congressmen. And all Nationalists.

'I would have thought their word counted for something.'

'Your own, I am sure, would be sufficient,' said Owen politely.

Labiba laughed drily.

'If I know Mahmoud, none of our words will be sufficient. He will want to check all.'

'As I say, he is merely checking possibilities.'

'But why check this poor boy? He is shattered enough as it is.'

'He has been spending a lot of time in the quarter, Madam Latifa. "Creeping around" is how they put it.'

'Have you never been lovelorn, Captain Owen?'

'Not to that extent.'

'Ah, but you are English, Captain Owen. You do not like to show your feelings as we Egyptians do. But I have persuaded you, I hope, about poor Suleiman?'

'It is not me you have to persuade, Mahmoud is in charge of the case.'

'Ah, yes, but since I had spoken to you previously about Suleiman, I thought – Have you had a chance to have a word with him on that score? I am still worried about him – even more worried now that I know how she died. He will be very angry, I fear. I am afraid he may do something rash.'

'That was not the occasion. I will, however, still try to see him.'

'Please do. He means no harm. Yet he may do some.'

'I will do my best. But the case is Mahmoud's.'

'Of course. I understand.' She paused. 'Have you spoken to Mahmoud lately?'

'I spoke to him yesterday.'

'Did you discuss with him –? You know I am interested in female circumcision.'

'We did not, in fact, discuss that.'

There was a little silence.

'You see, I felt there was a chance of him taking a line sympathetic to us.'

'I am sure he would not wish to take a line unsympathetic to you.'

'It is just that now that the case has become one of murder –'

'I am afraid that on that Mahmoud will have to speak for himself.'

'Of course. Of course. And you yourself, Captain Owen, you are still taking an interest?'

'In the wider sense, certainly.'

Paul had convened another meeting, this time at the Consulate. Owen had assumed it was a continuation of the one on the gravedigger dispute but when he got there he was surprised to see Macrae and Ferguson. Paul was looking grave.

'His Excellency has asked me to convene this meeting,' he said. 'It concerns a major complaint from the Khedive. We are to explore the circumstances and then draft a formal reply.'

There were two Ministers present, junior but Ministers. One of them was the man from the Department of Irrigation whom Owen had already met. The other was unfamiliar to him. He appeared to have something to do with the Khedive's Office.

'I understand,' said Paul, 'that the Khedive wishes the Consul-General to raise this directly with the British Foreign Secretary?'

'That is correct, yes,' said the man from the Khedive's Office.

'I would hope it needn't go so far. Perhaps if our meeting this morning is able to give the Khedive satisfaction –?'

'That would be desirable,' said the Minister, 'but it may not be enough. In view of the international implications.'

'International implications?' said Paul. 'But – ?'

'We view this as inconsistent with Treaty Obligations. Not to mention as constituting a grave insult to His Royal Highness.'

'I cannot tell you how desolate we all are at the Consulate-General,' said Paul. 'Nor how shocked and saddened we feel that such an incident should have occurred.'

'Plunder and pillage,' said the Minister.

'Exactly!' said Paul.

'Of the Khedive's own premises!'

'Incredible!' said Paul, shaking his head. 'Mamur Zapt?'

Jesus! thought Owen, frantically racking his memory.

'I understand you were there?'

'Well –'

'Not exactly there,' put in Ferguson helpfully. 'Nearby.'

'I was hoping you would be able to tell us what happened.'

'Well –'

'The regulator burst,' said Macrae. 'We had to take action.'

'Well, naturally,' said the man from the Khedive's Office.

'We had to fill in the breach. So I sent my men out –'

Light at last began to dawn.

'I cannot say how much I regret –' began Macrae.

'But the Khedive's own palace! The Khedive's own furniture!'

'A dreadful mistake!' said Paul.

'It was a wee laddie!' pleaded Macrae.

'New out here!' put in Ferguson.

'Dew still wet!' said Macrae.

'Have him beheaded!' said the Minister.

'Well –'

Paul was the first to recover.

'Certainly!' he snapped.

Ferguson and Macrae gaped.

'At once!' said the Minister.

Paul rubbed his chin.

'It would have to go to the Foreign Secretary. British.'

'None of your weak liberal nonsense!' warned the Minister.

'The last thing I had in mind,' said Paul.

Macrae found his voice.

'But, man, ye cannae –'

'Perhaps beheading would be too quick,' said the Minister thoughtfully. 'How about garotting?'

'The very thought that was going through my mind!' cried Paul.

'Jesus, man!' began Ferguson. 'Ye –'

'But too easy!' said Paul.

'There is that,' acknowledged the Minister.

'It would be over too quickly.'

'Torture?' suggested the Minister.

'It needs to be lingering,' said Paul, deep in thought. Suddenly he brightened. 'I know!' he said. 'The glasshouse!'

'Glass House?' said the Minister, interested. 'Well, that certainly sounds promising. Fried, you mean?'

'It's an old military punishment.'

'Ah, well, they would know. Judging from our experience of them.'

'Experts,' said Paul. 'Experts. But, look, there's a problem here. If it goes to the Foreign Secretary he may not agree.'

'Too liberal, you mean?'

'Exactly.'

'Perhaps,' said the Minister, 'on second thoughts, it might be best if it were handled locally.'

'Do you think that would satisfy the Khedive?'

'Oh, yes,' said the Minister, 'I think he would be very satisfied indeed. Glass House? Lingering? Oh, yes. Very satisfied.'

Macrae stayed behind after the Minister had left.

'Look, man,' he said to Paul, 'I know you mean well, but I don't trust those Army bastards –'

'Army?' said Paul. 'Who's talking about the Army? I'm thinking of him assisting the Consul-General's wife in their greenhouse.'

Owen could hear the pad-pad of bare feet coming along the corridor. A moment later the constable appeared with Babikr in tow. He pushed him into Owen's room and then took up position outside the door.

'I shall be standing here, little dove,' he said to Babikr,

'and if there's any trouble, I'll come in and beat the hell out of you.'

It was plain, though, that there was going to be no trouble. Babikr, lost and forlorn, stood bewildered in front of Owen.

Owen asked him how things were.

'Pretty well, Effendi,' he replied mechanically.

And, indeed, they were probably not all bad. You got regular meals, you were free from the usual back-breaking work of the fellah, and you could spend the day chatting to the other prisoners.

Babikr liked a good chat; but so far he had said nothing about his attempt to blow up the Manufiya Regulator. Owen knew that because he had put a spy in the cell with him.

He had decided to try a different approach.

'Your friends at the barrage are well,' he said. Babikr nodded acknowledgement. 'But they do not send you greetings. They will not come and see you. Why is that, Babikr?'

In fact, the workmen would have come and seen him but Owen had prevented them.

Babikr flinched slightly.

'I do not know,' he said.

'It is because they do not understand you. They do not understand how you could have done a thing like this. Were you not one of them? Did you not work together? Had you not stood side by side when the sun was hot and the work hard? They thought they could count on you, Babikr. They thought they knew you.'

He waited. Babikr shuffled his feet unhappily.

'But they did not know you, Babikr. They could not have known you if all the time you meditated such things. Can this be the Babikr we thought we knew, they ask? And they are bewildered. They cannot understand how this could be. They say, if we only knew why he had done this thing, then, perhaps, we could understand.'

Babikr stood there miserably, head lowered.

'Why did you do it, Babikr?'

He waited, but Babikr did not reply.

'That you did it is a bad thing. For that you must pay. But you must have had a reason, and if your friends knew that reason, then perhaps their hearts would not be so wounded. You had friends among them, Babikr. Can you not speak to them?'

'No, I cannot,' said Babikr in a low voice.

'You have shamed them. They have to live with that shame. If they knew why you had done it, perhaps that would help them. Can you not help them, Babikr?'

Owen could see that the man was feeling the words keenly; but still he would not speak.

'They say, perhaps it was against us that he acted. Perhaps in his heart he hated us. Perhaps we have done wrong things.'

'No, no!' said Babikr. 'No!'

'Or against Macrae Effendi. Or Ferguson Effendi.'

'No.'

'Then why, Babikr? No one does a thing like this without reason. Could you tell them the reason? You have left a hole in their hearts, Babikr. Could you not at least make easy the wound?'

'I cannot,' said the man, distressed.

'Why not? I refuse to believe, Babikr, that you are unfeeling to your friends.'

'Effendi, I am not. Believe me, I am not!'

'Well, Babikr, I will tell them that. That, at least, they will be glad to know.'

'Thank you, Effendi,' said the man brokenly.

'But cannot you tell them more?'

'Believe me, Effendi, I cannot. I would, but –'

'What is it that stops you?'

Babikr shook his head in misery.

'Is it that you are not alone in this? That you think of others? That,' said Owen with sudden inspiration, 'you are perhaps bound to them?'

'I have sworn an oath,' said the man, in a low voice.

Owen considered for a moment. This was where it could go wrong.

'Then I can understand you,' he said at last, gently. 'May I tell your friends that, Babikr? That you had sworn an oath?'

'You may, Effendi. I would be glad if you would.'

'I will. But, Babikr, some oaths are good, some bad. They

will want to be sure that this was a good oath. What shall I tell them?'

'Tell them I was beholden.'

'Ah, it was something you owed?'

'Yes, Effendi.'

'To a man, or to men?'

Babikr looked him straight in the face and shook his head.

Owen knew that, for the moment, he had taken it as far as he could.

He was still sitting there thinking it over when Yussef, his orderly, announced that there was someone who wished to see him. Owen knew from this that he was an ordinary Arab. Most others, that is to say, those who were not Arabs or who did not think of themselves as ordinary, described themselves as effendi. Effendi wishing to see Owen usually presented themselves directly to Nikos, the Mamur Zapt's official clerk. The ordinary Arab, abashed by the huge facade of the Bab-el-Khalk, lingered outside on the steps until he could pluck up enough courage to accost an orderly, who would, in lordly fashion, instruct him to wait outside the orderly room until his betters decided what to do with him.

The man, when Yussef brought him along, confirmed Owen's assumption. Almost. He was not the lowest of the low for his dress was of good cloth. The white turban bound round his tarboosh, for example, was of cashmere. But he was wearing a turban and not the pot-like tarboosh by itself, which would have been the mark of the effendi; and he was wearing a galabeeyah not a suit.

Owen rose to greet him and led him across to the two canework chairs put beneath the window where there was a chance of catching a breath of air. The windows were shuttered against the sun but through the slats there occasionally crept a waft of something which was not entirely tepid.

Yussef hovered for a moment outside the door. Owen knew why. He was wondering whether the man merited coffee. Evidently he decided that he did, for a little later Owen heard the pad of returning feet and smelt the coffee. That in itself was significant, for Yussef's judgement in these matters was usually fine. All the same there was something about the man that was slightly puzzling, something that Owen was not familiar with.

His name, he said, was Al-Sayyid Hannam, and he had come about his son.

'You are Suleiman's father?'

'Yes.' He sighed. 'And sometimes I wonder what I have done.'

'All fathers do that.'

'All fathers have hopes for their sons; and when they see themselves disappointed, they ask themselves why.'

'Sometimes it is mere youthfulness.'

'That is what I told myself. When this foolish business of the girl first came up.'

'You knew about it?'

The man nodded.

'Suleiman, since he came up to the city, has been staying with the family of a business friend of mine. When he learned what was happening he was troubled and spoke to me. I said: "Let it be. The boy is young. It will come to nothing." But that was before I knew who or what she was.'

'A water-carrier's daughter?'

'That would be bad enough. For I had set my hopes higher. I had sent my son to the city in the hope that he would do better than his father.' He looked at Owen. 'Not that I am complaining. God has smiled on me and I have prospered. But I work the land. Our family has always worked the land. Well, that is good; but it is hard work and a father always wants better for his boy. I had friends and they found him a place with the Water Board. It is a good job, I told him: water is a thing of the future as well as a thing of the past, and you will rise with the future.'

'And so he has,' said Owen, 'if what he told me is true.'

'I say nothing against him at work. It is when he is not at work that I am troubled.'

Owen was used to people discussing their family problems with him. Yussef did; his barber did; Nuri Pasha did; all Egyptians did. It was the principal subject of conversation, taking the place of the weather in England. He wondered, however, if Suleiman's father knew where things had got to.

'You have doubtless heard,' he said, 'what has befallen the girl?'

'I have heard she is dead. Well, that is bad, and, although her father may not believe it of me, I grieve for him. I grieve for my son, too, for I cannot believe that his love was anything but honourable. Foolish, perhaps, but not dishonourable. All the same, mixed with my grief, is a certain relief.'

'You have heard of what she died?'

The man nodded.

'I have heard two things. The first is terrible, but must be as God wills. It is about the second that I have come.'

'What have you heard?'

'That the girl was strangled. And that my son is suspected.'

'I would not go so far as that. The Parquet suspects all until they are proved innocent. That is how it is with your son. He is suspected neither more nor less.'

'Nevertheless he is suspected? Well, my friend was right. It is time I came.'

'There are powerful people who speak for him.'

The old man smiled.

'But not as powerful as the Mamur Zapt.'

He had come in the time-honoured way to plead for his son. And in the time-honoured way he had gone to the Mamur Zapt, not for justice, for that was the prerogative of the Kadi, but for mercy, because that was the prerogative of power, and for centuries the Mamur Zapt had been the Khedive's right-hand man, the man, after him, most powerful in the city. Things had, of course, changed; but many in the countryside were not yet aware of this.

'The time for intercession is not yet,' he said. 'It may be that there will be no need of it. The Law has still to ask the questions.'

'In the asking,' said Suleiman's father, 'lies danger.'

'The man who asks,' said Owen, 'is a man of honour. But perhaps it would be well to find another man of law who can watch over your son and advise him.'

'I have already done that. It is not that. It is –' he hesitated – 'that the questions could go deep.'

'Why should they go deep?'

'Because these things have roots. There is bad blood between me and the girl's father.'

'Why should that affect your son?'

'It already has affected him. It was why the girl's father spurned him. If there had not been bad blood, perhaps none of this would ever have happened. That is why I wonder what I have done.'

'You should not blame yourself. One cannot trace these things to their infinite cause. All these things are past.'

'I wish they were,' said the old man. 'I wish they were. It was never my intention – but sometimes these things return upon us.'

'How came it that there was bad blood between you?'

'We came from the same village. We worked fields next to each other. There was a dispute between us over water. I thought I was in the right, he thought he was. We went to a kadi, who ruled in my favour.'

The old man shrugged.

'Bitter words were said. I was young and hot and enforced the law to the letter. It meant he went without water. He had to leave the village. It was the beginning for me. Afterwards, I prospered so that now I own more land than the entire village used to hold. But for him, it seems, it was the end –'

'It was as God decreed.'

'But sometimes He works these things out to their infinite end and lets justice fall not on us but on our children. That is what I am afraid of.'

'Who can read God's pattern?' said Owen.

The debate was not going well for the Government. The Minister had found himself unexpectedly under fire. He would certainly get his Supplementary Vote – the Government had an enormous majority in the Assembly – but things were proving stickier than he had expected.

'This is a work of national importance,' he said indignantly.

A man rose on the benches opposite.

'No one doubts that,' he said. 'It is the cost of the proposals that we are disputing.'

Since it was unusual for the Opposition to want to reduce the cost of anything – they were normally in favour of increasing it – the Minister was slightly taken aback. He muttered something about technical reasons.

'But that is precisely the point!' said the man opposite. 'We are being asked to take these technical arguments on trust. Has an independent opinion been sought?'

'Tenders will be invited in the normal way,' said the Minister.

'But who has drawn up the specifications?'

'The Department's own advisers –'

'British. And the contract will go to the British. Has consideration been given to asking independent consultants to draw up the specifications?'

'That would increase the cost.'

'It would probably reduce costs. The Department's estimates are usually inflated. Why will not the Minister go outside the Department for advice? Outside the country, even? This is a very big contract and firms outside the country will be interested.'

'They will have an opportunity of tendering.'

'But on terms drawn up by the Department's British advisers. That is what we are objecting to.'

It was the usual Nationalist tactic. They wanted the British out; and while they certainly didn't want other countries in, internationalism was a handy stick to beat the Government with.

'Those estimates are pared to the bone!' whispered Macrae, beside Owen, indignantly. 'That laddie doesn't know what he's talking about. Who is he?'

'Mohammed Jubbara,' whispered Owen. 'He's a big man in the Nationalist Party.'

The Minister was muttering something about The Time Factor.

'This is an emergency,' he proclaimed.

Someone else rose on the benches opposite.

'Hamad el Sid,' whispered Owen.

'I hope the Government, in its eagerness to do a quick deal with foreign business interests, will think about the effect of its grandiose schemes on the poor.'

'We are always thinking of the poor,' said the Minister.

'And how to grind them down further, I know,' said Hamad el Sid.

The Minister affected shock. He turned to his colleagues on the benches behind him.

'The schemes that Mr el Sid so disparages have increased the production of grain three times; the production of cotton five times; the production of –'

'But at a price,' interrupted Hamad el Sid, 'in terms of the health of the poor. Is the Minister aware that the incidence of bilharzia and ankylostoma in the male population of Egypt is now eighty-five per cent? Would he care to put a figure – since he is so keen on figures – on the role of water-borne diseases over the last few years? And relate them to the public works of which he is so proud?'

It was almost, thought Owen, as if he had been talking to Cairns-Grant. Perhaps he had; or perhaps Cairns-Grant had been talking to him.

Macrae shifted restlessly.

'Aye,' he said, 'but –'

The Nationalists shifted back again.

Was it true, a third man wanted to know –

'Al-Faqih Mas'udi,' whispered Owen.

'– that the proposed new regulator will take up a substantial part of the remarkable gardens at the barrage. Gardens which were a source of pride and pleasure to so many ordinary citizens of Cairo –'

And so it went on. At one point Owen took Macrae and Ferguson out for a cup of coffee. In the corridor he saw Labiba Latifa. She waved a hand to him.

'We're having a meeting. Care to join us?' she said.

'Thanks. I've got my own,' said Owen.

Back in the Chamber, Members were debating the effects of the Aswan Barrage on the Temple at Philae.

'What has this got to do with replacing the Manufiya Regulator?' pleaded the Minister despairingly.

At last it was over and the Supplementary Vote, despite the Minister's travails, agreed. Macrae and Ferguson were jubilant.

'That means we can get on with it?'

'Heavens, no!' said Owen. 'Now it has to go to London.'

'But – but – that will take years!'

'Aye,' said Owen.

A door opened and out popped Zeinab.

Owen was astounded. She had hitherto shown absolutely no interest in the workings of parliamentary democracy. Power was one thing and she was interested in that, but parliamentary democracy, especially in Egypt, quite another. She was a true daughter of her father. Nuri Pasha had once been a Minister; indeed, had hopes, though they were receding, of being one again. But he knew that this had nothing to do with so unreliable a thing as voting. It was a matter of securing the Khedive's favour. That, in Zeinab's view, was what Government was all about.

'What are you doing here?'

'I have been at a meeting.'

That was another shaker. Women didn't go to meetings in Egypt, certainly not at the National Assembly. Even if they were, as Zeinab was, dressed in black from head to foot and heavily veiled. Except that . . .

'Labiba?' he said.

Zeinab nodded.

'Circumcision?'

'Certainly not! In the Assembly? They would be shocked!'

'I meant are you talking about circumcision? Is that the subject of the meeting?'

'They would still be shocked. No, health. Sub-heading (very small letters): women's health. That gets rid of the old dodderers, who would otherwise come to hear how their heart was getting on. It does, admittedly, attract some rather strange men, but Labiba is firm with them.'

'Is she chairing?'

'No, that Scotsman is. You know, the one who cuts you up.'

'Cairns-Grant?'

'Probably. He has a workman's hands. But then he would.'

'How's the meeting going?'

'It's coming to an end soon. I thought I would leave early as the man next to me is getting too excited.'

'I don't blame him,' said Owen, glancing along the corridor. No one was coming. He put his arm round her.

'Not here!' said Zeinab, alarmed.

The door of the committee room opened again and they quietly disengaged. Out came Mohammed Jubbara, Hamad el Sid and al-Faqih Mas'udi. Owen wasn't sure whether they had seen. Behind them, close behind, was Suleiman. His eyes were burning.

Mas'udi stopped.

'Can I get you an arabeah?' he said to Zeinab.

'No thank you. I have a word or two I want to say to the Mamur Zapt,' she replied sweetly.

Mas'udi gave him a startled look.

Back at her *apartment* Zeinab did, indeed, have a word or two to say.

'You have an unhealthy mind,' she concluded severely, 'in an over-healthy body.'

Out at the barrage little clumps of papyrus were spiralling in the sun. When they neared the barrage they wavered for a moment uncertainly and then accelerated in towards the piers. Just before they reached them, they were sucked downwards and lost in the grating.

In the shallows of the river's edge two men were loading building water-skins on to a donkey. When they had finished, they led it up on to the bank. One of them put a large hamper-like wicker basket on top of the water-skins and then perched himself above that. The other man gave the donkey a thwack on the flank.

The noise startled the doves in the palms and they fluttered agitatedly. They were all right, thought Owen. It was the ones in the basket that needed to worry.

He followed the donkey up into the Gardens. There were fewer people there than on his previous visits; or perhaps it was that, with the sun now almost directly overhead, they had retreated into the shade.

Over towards the regulator, Ferguson was ominously busy with white tape and a measuring rod. He waved to Owen as he went past.

The workmen, as Owen had hoped, were having lunch. He squatted down beside them at the tray.

'You here again?'

'Babikr asked me to send you greetings.'

The men received them in silence. Although Owen had embroidered a little when he was talking to Babikr, he had probably reflected their feelings.

'He asked me to tell you he had sworn an oath.'

The men looked up.

'An oath, was it?'

It did not excuse, but did explain.

'Yes. He said he was beholden.'

'Ah!'

They went back to their eating.

'I think better of him,' said Owen, 'but still I am worried.'

He knew they were listening.

'Why is that?' one of them said.

'Well, what sort of oath is it that dare not declare itself?'

'A bad oath,' someone said.

'That is exactly what I thought. And then I thought: where does a bad oath stop?'

'It's stopped so far as Babikr is concerned,' said someone.

'For the moment. But where does the man who exacted the oath want it to stop? Why cannot he come forward and tell us the extent of the oath?'

'If it was a bad oath, perhaps he is afraid,' volunteered someone.

'That is what leaves me afraid,' said Owen. 'And so I ask: to whom has he sworn the oath? Is there one of you who could tell me?'

They shook their heads. That did not surprise Owen. Nor did it trouble him. No one would wish to do it openly, but they

107

might well come later in private, whether as an individual or after the group had consulted among itself. As they had done before.

'You see,' he said, 'if it has not stopped, further harm could befall. To Babikr. To us all.'

'Yes,' said Georgiades, 'but you've never given *me* flowers.'

'You don't look like a flower person to me,' said the gardener, inspecting him critically.

'I've got a wife, haven't I?'

The two had become great buddies. They were sitting on the edge of a gadwal drinking the gardener's tea, which, with Eastern hospitality, he had also offered to Owen.

'Perhaps I will give you flowers,' said the gardener, relenting.

'You gave some to Babikr,' Georgiades pointed out.

'Not *to* Babikr; *for* Babikr. For him to give to another.'

'Ah, there's a woman in it, is there? And not his wife. For his wife stays in the village.' Georgiades shook his head sorrowfully. 'That a man like you should encourage vice!'

'I did not encourage vice,' said the gardener, stung. 'I merely gave him some flowers. For which he paid me ten milliemes.'

'Without knowing who they were going to? They might have been going to the Lizard Man for all you know!'

'They were *not* going to the Lizard Man!'

'Are you sure? I wouldn't rule it out. Babikr was a friend of the Lizard Man, wasn't he?'

'He had other friends as well.'

'Up here in the city?'

'Look,' said the gardener, 'I know who the flowers were for and it wasn't the Lizard Man!'

'Whisper it to me,' challenged Georgiades, 'and I'll believe you.'

The gardener opened his mouth.

Then closed it again.

Firmly.

'If I tell you,' he said, 'the Lizard Man might hear me!'

8

One of the sights of Cairo was the water-carts. Every morning and sometimes at other points during the day they would go through the streets dampening down the dust. There was a tank at the back of the cart from which the water would spray out in little fountains. Urchins would dart in and out under the jets and after the cart had passed there would be a brief moment when the air was full of the seaside smell of water on hot sand. Cairenes loved that moment. They would come out into the doorways and sniff the air like dogs.

There was a water-cart ahead of Owen now. But it was not spraying the streets. It was standing at a corner and a group of water-carriers were filling their bags from the tank.

'They won't want to do that next week,' Owen said to the driver as he passed. 'Not when there's water in the canal. What will you do then?'

'Old man Fayoum will just move it further into the Gamaliya,' said one of the water-carriers.

'Ah, it belongs to Omar Fayoum?'

'It certainly does. And they say he's going to get another like it soon.'

'He must be doing well, then.'

'Never done better, he says. The last few months especially. Though I don't know how that could be. It's the same water, isn't it? And it takes the same time to carry.'

'Ah, but does it?' said the man next to him, stooping to pick up his skins.

'What do you mean?' asked Owen.

'Well, they do say he's found another place where he can get it.'

'That's a lot of nonsense!' said someone standing on the other side of the cart. Owen couldn't see him clearly but thought it might be Ahmed Uthman, the husband of the woman who had taken Leila in.

'It's all got to come from the river, hasn't it?' said a man beside him. Owen could see him. It was Leila's father.

'Well, that's more than we know,' said the water-carrier who had first spoken.

'You don't know very much, then!' retorted Ahmed Uthman.

'What's the trouble?' said the driver of the cart. 'Don't you like our water?'

'I like the water. It's the price I don't like.'

'Well, you don't have to pay it, then, do you?' said the driver. 'Tell him, Ahmed!'

'Why don't you just bugger off?' said Ahmed Uthman, coming round the side of the cart.

'Yes,' said Leila's father, joining him. 'Why don't you?'

'Here, what's going on?'

'You don't like the water? You don't have to have it, then!'

'Well, I won't! Not if it's like that!'

'We won't need to, will we? Not after the Cut!' said his friend, supporting him.

'We don't like your water, either,' said Leila's father. 'Wherever it comes from. We don't want to see it in the Gamaliya!'

'I take my water where I like!'

'Oh, do you? Well, in that case – '

He moved forward threateningly.

Suddenly, he saw Owen.

'Ahmed, it's him!' he said.

'Him!'

Ahmed Uthman recovered first.

'Get out of here!' he shouted to the driver. 'Quick!'

The driver seized his whip. Ahmed Uthman and Leila's father threw their bags into the cart and leaped up after them. The cart shot away.

'You watch out!' shouted Leila's father to the two water-carriers as they lurched away.

'We'll be looking out for you!' called Ahmed Uthman.

The two water-carriers stood there for a moment, dazed.

'What's all this about?'

'I don't know. Why do they have to be like that?'

'Ahmed Uthman's always like that. But what's got into Ali Khedri?'

'It's his daughter, I suppose.'

'He never cared two milliemes about his daughter! All he cared about was getting a job in that cart!'

'Well, that's gone, hasn't it? Omar Fayoum won't be interested in him now. Now that he's not going to marry the girl.'

'She's well out of it, that's what I say. Or would be if she wasn't dead.'

'She may well be. Do you know what Marriam said to me? She said, I'd rather be dead than marry that dirty old bastard!'

'Ah, well, it's one thing saying that – '

The two men shouldered their skins and walked away.

Owen hesitated for a moment and then ran after them.

'Your pardon, friends,' he said. 'I fear that I may have brought that on you!'

'No pardon needed,' they said courteously. 'We brought it on ourselves. Though quite why – '

'They did not like it when you spoke of where Omar Fayoum gets his water from.'

'Up to some fiddle, I expect!'

'Where *does* he get it from?'

'He doesn't always go to the river for it, that's for certain. What do you think, Selim?'

'Well, I wouldn't be surprised if he goes into the es-Zakir and gets it out of the pond.'

The other man laughed.

'He'd have to have something worked out with the gardeners.'

'I wouldn't put that past him.'

He looked at Owen.

'You're not supposed to take it out of the ponds,' he explained. 'Nor any other place where there's stagnant water.

Not these days. They say it's not clean enough. Not for drinking. Though what Omar Fayoum is supposed to do and what he does are two different things.'

Owen was, as it happens, on his way to the Gamaliya. He wanted to make another attempt at a peaceful resolution of the dispute between the Muslim gravediggers and the Jews. The adjourned meeting had not resumed; but Paul and Owen, happening to meet up with McPhee in the bar of the Sporting Club, had agreed to try something out on the two sides.

McPhee was going to tell the Jews sternly that they could do the Cut, as it was their turn, but for no extra money. If the fact that it was the Sabbath ruled it out for them, then the Muslims would do it.

Owen, meanwhile, was going to talk to the Muslims, equally sternly, and tell them that it had been decided to return to the traditional arrangements for the Cut, that the Jews would do the cutting as it was their turn, but for no extra pay, and that if they didn't like it, then the task would be offered to the Muslims. If there was any difficulty from them then British soldiers would do it.

The theory was that the prospect of the Jews declining would keep the Muslims happy, while the agonizing that the Jews would have to do over their decision would keep them, if not exactly happy, then at least preoccupied. With any luck both sides would dangle until the very last moment, until, in fact, it was too late for either of them to cause much trouble.

Thus the theory; not quite, at once, as simple in practice.

'Suppose they don't refuse?' the Muslim gravediggers objected. 'Suppose the buggers agree to do it after all?'

'Well, then, they have to do it. It's their turn.'

'I don't agree with this turn business,' said one of the gravediggers. 'Why have they got to have a turn at all?'

'Because it's always been like that' – normally a clinching argument in Cairo – 'and because it's too late to change now.'

'We can do it as well as they can!'

'I'm sure you can. That is why we do it in turn. One year it's you, the next year it's them. This year it's them.'

112

'Yes, but this is the last year. We're going to lose out.'

'You don't lose out. This is when it happens to stop.'

'Yes, but if it stopped *next* year, then they'd be the ones to lose out!'

'No one's losing out. You've –' a sudden moment of inspiration – 'you've both done it an equal number of times!'

They looked at each other, thunder-struck.

'That so?'

'Absolutely!'

No one was in a position to contradict. They subsided, grumbling.

But then returned.

'Yes, but it wouldn't have stopped if it hadn't been for them, would it?'

'What do you mean?'

'Putting that girl there. That made it all wrong.'

'That's got nothing to do with it. Nor have the Jews, either. It was the Government that decided to end the Cut. For very good reasons, too. That land is a health hazard.'

Help arrived from an unexpected quarter.

'I don't think putting the girl there would have made it *wrong*, Mustapha,' said one of the gravediggers diffidently. 'It would have made it sweet, surely?'

'Well, it would have if it had been one of their girls. But it was one of ours. I mean, you can't have that, can you?'

'The girl has got nothing to do with it!' said Owen with emphasis. 'Her death has got nothing whatsoever to do with the Cut. And she was not killed by the Jews!'

'Who was she killed by, then?' asked one of the men.

'We don't quite know that yet,' Owen had to admit. 'But we do know that she was not killed by the Jews.'

'If we could be sure of that,' said one of the more thoughtful gravediggers.

On his way back to the Ezbekiya, where he was meeting Zeinab, Owen cut across the Quartier Rosetti, and in doing so crossed the line of the Khalig Canal. To his surprise, down among the rubbish he saw Mahmoud.

'Hello,' he called. 'What's all this?'

Mahmoud looked up, saw him, and, with a certain amount of relief, climbed out and came towards him.

'I'm retracing the line that must have been taken with her body,' he said. 'It's a hell of a long way. She couldn't have run there, as I had thought.'

'It's a long way to carry that sort of weight,' said Owen, looking up the length of the Canal. 'Not to mention the risk of being seen.'

'That's why he would have gone along the Canal,' said Mahmoud. 'It was dark, too.'

'He'd have had to have known what he was doing to walk along the Canal in the dark.'

The bed was choked with rubbish.

'That is what I am finding,' said Mahmoud drily.

Owen offered to walk with him. He wasn't meeting Zeinab till seven o'clock.

Their way led at first past the backs of some old Mameluke mansions with entrances on the Sharia Es-Sureni. Seeing them from the rear like this was a revelation because while from the front they looked solid and austere, from the back they were a riot of sixteenth century fantasy. Beautiful staircases dropped down to the canal, where, presumably, there would once have been boats, while above them rose meshrebiya oriels and pergola'ed terraces, feathery with palms and green with creepers.

They were once the most prized of houses and this the most prized of aspects. He thought of Venice but it was a Venice of the desert, where water was treasured and the stuff of paradise; almost literally so, for paradise was the old Arabic word for garden, a vision of shade and green and fertility among the heat and sand, oasis in the desert.

Now, though, the houses were decaying and crumbling, the staircases slippery with slime. The heavy, box-like windows overhanging the water let mosquitoes in through their fretwork and the stench alone was enough to drive their occupants into the rooms at the front of the houses.

Below the staircases, along the side of the canal, heavy, metal, distinctly unmedieval pipes ran for part of the way, themselves often covered by fallen masonry or rotten vegetation.

They were picking their way along the bed of the canal, past falls of rubble, slides of earth and sand, drifts of kitchen leavings and the occasional carcass, when they suddenly saw someone ahead of them. He turned to greet them as they came up. It was young Suleiman.

'You see,' he said, 'here I am again.'

'What is it this time?'

'The same. I'm checking the pipes.' He made a gesture of despair. 'In so far as I can check them under all this stuff.'

'Don't you have instruments?'

'We do. They show there's a big water loss in this part of the system. We want to get it sorted out before we bring the new pipes in.'

'You know the canal well?'

'This part of it.' He sniffed. 'Too well.'

He was looking all the time at Mahmoud, seemed, in fact, almost to be avoiding looking directly at Owen. Owen thought this strange, since Mahmoud was the one who was pressing hardest. Something seemed to be bothering him with respect to Owen. Was it Zeinab? Had he seen them outside the Committee Room in the National Assembly? Had it offended his prudishness? Or his feelings about Arab and Englishman? Whatever it was, it made it difficult for Owen to have a fatherly talk with him.

'What do you think about it?' Suleiman said suddenly to Mahmoud. 'This business of female circumcision?'

'Well, I –' said Mahmoud, taken aback.

'Labiba thinks you might be sympathetic to our cause.'

'I am sympathetic,' said Mahmoud, after a moment's thought. 'But it has to be a separate thing from my work.'

'You're a member of the Nationalist Party, aren't you? Labiba says the younger members are beginning to understand that circumcision is bad. She says it will take time, but if the key younger ones are convinced, then a Nationalist Government of the future will take action.'

'There will be a lot of things on which they will have to take action,' said Mahmoud, neutrally but not unsympathetically.

He and Owen continued on their way. It was, as Mahmoud

115

had said, a long way. And difficult to negotiate, even in daylight. Even more so in the dark. You would, indeed, have to know the canal well.

Owen was expecting Mahmoud to refer to this again. Instead, he said:

'Why carry her this far? He must have had some reason. You know,' he said, 'I am beginning to change my mind. I am almost beginning to think there could be some connection with the Cut, after all.'

When they emerged from the canal, just by the temporary earth dam which divided the canal from the river, and where the Cut was to be made, Owen found the scene very different from when he had last visited it. Everywhere, brightly-coloured pavilions had sprung up, many of them walled round by little carpeted fences to form enclosures within which patrons could sit. Sellers of sweets, pastries, peanuts and sugar cane were marking off their pitches. Boats hung with bunting were already crowding about the entrance to the canal on the river side of the dam. And there were people everywhere, some of them workmen, many of them vendors, most of them simply onlookers getting in the way.

There was a great mass of people down in the bed of the canal pressing in round the foot of the giant earth cone. Over their heads Owen could see McPhee, large, pink, determined, and around him a ring of constables. He looked up and saw Owen.

'Ah, Owen, pleased to see you. Very pleased.'

Owen forced a way through the throng.

'What's the trouble?'

McPhee pointed down to the foot of the cone.

'This!'

The earth had been scraped away in what looked like the start of a small burrow, the sort of thing a rabbit might have made, if, of course, there had been any rabbits.

'I don't see the problem.'

'What made it?'

'A dog?'

'What for?'

116

'Well, Christ, I don't know. A bone?'

'Or several. They think another woman's been buried here.'

'It's just a dog!'

'They think it's smelt it.'

'Well, is that bloody likely?'

'They think so. The first one was taken out, they say, so another one has been put there.'

'It's the Jews,' said someone in the crowd.

'We're going to have to dig,' said McPhee. 'To show them.'

Owen nodded.

'Right.' He raised his voice. 'The Bimbashi and I are sure there is no one buried under here. But just to show you, and set your minds at rest, we are going to dig. Now, are any of you good at –?'

A man shouldered forward.

'Effendi, I am an expert!'

Owen recognized one of the Muslim gravediggers.

'Just the man! Any more like you?'

Several fellahin eagerly came forward.

'Spades?'

The constables cleared some space, linked arms and then leaned back against the crowd. The crowd supported them happily, craning over their shoulders to get a better look.

The gravedigger seized the first spade and began work enthusiastically.

'Allah, what strength!' said the crowd appreciatively.

The gravedigger, preening, redoubled his efforts.

'What need is there for more when we have men who can work like this?' asked Owen rhetorically.

'What need for Jews?' said the gravedigger over his shoulder.

'Is that the place where the other was found?' asked Mahmoud, who had pushed his way through to join Owen.

'The very place!' chorused the crowd.

'I thought it was round the other side,' said one of the constables doubtfully.

Mahmoud turned to him.

'You were here?'

'Yes, Effendi. I was at the station when they reported it. I came with the Mamur.'

'And you think it was round the other side?'

'I'm pretty sure, Effendi. And it wasn't really under the mound. It was more beside it.'

'Whereabouts?'

The constable extended an arm and pointed.

'Under their feet?'

The crowd on that side moved back in consternation.

'Yes, Effendi.'

'Abdul, I don't like standing here!' said an alarmed voice. 'Suppose the ground opens?'

'Well, then, you'd bloody fall in!' said the constable.

'But then if there's another body there – '

'It'd be over here,' said Owen, annoyed. 'This damned dog is not a gold-miner.'

'Just watch it!' said McPhee. 'We don't want the whole cone coming down!'

'Not on us, we don't!' said the constables, pressing back harder against the crowd, which had now grown to fill the whole bed. At the sides, men were climbing on to each others' backs in order to see better. Above them, the bank of the Canal was lined yards-deep with people.

The gravedigger's spade struck something hard.

'Bone!' shouted the crowd.

The gravedigger plunged his hand in before Mahmoud could stop him.

'Stone!' he said disgustedly, producing it.

Disillusioned, he stood aside to let the others take over.

'Guide them!' said Owen. 'We don't want the cone falling in.'

'It takes an expert,' said the gravedigger modestly.

'If the body was found beside the cone,' Mahmoud asked the constable, 'why were they digging there?'

'It's the way they dig,' said the constable. 'They dig around it and pile the earth on top.'

'How was the body lying?'

'I didn't look too closely,' said the constable. 'It was all bulged up. Like a camel's belly.'

'Why was it swollen? Had it been lying in water?'

'There had been water. Because they're always digging out

the bed at this place, the bed is deeper here than elsewhere and the water lies longer.'

'So she could have been thrown into water?'

'Yes, Effendi.'

'Not buried at all?'

The crowd had been hearing this.

'Not buried at all?'

'Just thrown there,' said Mahmoud. 'It could have been anywhere.'

'Just like the Jews!' said the gravedigger. 'Couldn't even make a good job of it!'

'It wasn't the Jews,' said Mahmoud. 'It was some bad man.'

The crowd was clearly disappointed. The diggers who had also heard, began to lose heart.

'How about someone else having a go?' said one over his shoulder. No one seemed very willing.

Even the Muslim gravedigger was beginning to doubt.

'How long are we going to go on doing this, then?' he grumbled.

'Until we have set people's minds at rest,' said Owen sternly.

The gravedigger heaved out a few more half-hearted spadefuls.

'I think their minds are pretty well at rest now,' he said.

'No,' said Owen, 'we must go on until all are satisfied. All night if necessary.'

'All night?' said the gravedigger. 'Look – '

'Unless,' said Owen, looking around, 'those knowledgable –?'

The front ranks of the crowd, who had been standing there longest, decided that they were knowledgable enough and began to drift away.

'No woman,' said one of them as he left. 'That's a bit of a disappointment.'

'Well, you can't strike lucky all the time,' said his neighbour.

'We didn't even strike lucky that first time,' said the man, 'if what that Effendi said was true.'

'No,' agreed the neighbour despondently.

Owen, hearing, was very satisfied.

Mahmoud turned to him.

'I must go now,' he said. 'I've got to get back to the Gamaliya. There's someone I want to see.'

'Who's that?'

'The father. It was someone known to her, remember.'

There was still a small knot of people around McPhee. As he was passing, Owen heard one of them say:

'Well, then, if it wasn't a woman, what was it?'

'It wasn't anything,' said McPhee reassuringly. 'Just some animal.'

'Why would an animal want to dig holes in the "Bride"?'

'I don't know. It was probably just a dog.'

'It didn't look like a dog to me. They don't dig burrows. What do you think, Ahmed?'

'It looked more like the thing a lizard would dig.'

'Too big. Except – '

The thought struck them both at the same time.

'A lizard man!'

Owen took an arabeah up to the Ismailiya, where he was meeting Zeinab for lunch. Not in an Arab restaurant – they looked askance at women, even Pashas' daughters – but in a French one. Zeinab liked to eat French as well as dress French. She even normally spoke French, and she and Owen drifted in and out of French and English as the occasion arose. The culture of the Egyptian upper class was heavily French and there was as great a gap between it and that of the ordinary Egyptian as there was between the massive dams the British were erecting and, well, the Lizard Man.

Zeinab, however, was anti-French today. She had some intellectual periodicals under her arm, French, but different from the ones she usually took. She tapped one of them significantly.

'Napoleon was against women,' she said darkly. 'I've been reading.'

'Well, yes, but you've got to make allowances for the time.'

Zeinab took no notice.

'It's in the Code Napoléon,' she said.

Which was still the basis of the Egyptian legal code. When the Khedive Ismail had wanted to reform and modernize the Egyptian legal system he had simply adopted the Code wholesale.

'I don't think you can blame him entirely,' objected Owen. 'Islamic law – '

Zeinab brooded.

'Islamic law is men's law,' she said. 'The trouble is, when you turn to the alternative, what do you find? Men's law.'

'Law is the same for everyone,' said Owen. 'If you commit a murder, you get hanged for it. Never mind whether you're a man or a woman.'

'Yes, but some things affect women more than they do men.'

'Have you been talking to Labiba Latifa?' demanded Owen.

'Circumcision, for instance,' said Zeinab.

'That's social practice, not law. Why don't you talk to Mahmoud?'

'I will,' said Zeinab.

Owen had not intended to go back to the Gamaliya that day but when he returned to his office, he found Georgiades waiting for him. He had found out, he thought, the person whom Babikr had gone to see.

'He's a fiki,' he said. 'Several of the workmen go and see him. He used to live at their village but when he got old, he moved up here to be with his son. They still remember him in the village, and when the men come up here for the Inundation, they always take him something.'

'A fiki?' said Owen. 'Then he might know of the oath, even if it wasn't to him.'

A fiki was a professional reader, or singer, of the Koran and as a person of (some) learning and (some) holiness was the sort of person you might go to if you wanted a witness of authority when you were swearing an oath.

He lived in a small back street in the Gamaliya not far from the mosque. The son, slightly startled, showed them in.

'It is,' Owen explained, 'to do with a man known to you, who used to listen to you in your village.'

The fiki nodded.

'The men come to you, I know, each year when they are up here for the Inundation, bringing greetings from the village.'

The fiki nodded again.

'Was Babikr among them?'

'Babikr!' said the fiki.

'You know?'

'I know.'

'Was he among those who came to you?'

The fiki thought for a moment.

'Yes.'

'I wondered if he had talked of an oath?'

The fiki thought again.

'I do not think so.'

'It might have been one he had taken in the village. Do you recall such an oath?'

'He took various oaths. All do.'

'Do you remember the substance of the oaths?'

'To do with wedding settlements. There was an ox once, I think. These were the usual foolish disputes.'

'Do you recall them?'

'They are not worth recalling.'

'Yet Babikr, I think, was not a man to take them lightly.'

'He was not,' agreed the fiki. He warmed slightly. 'He was ever true to his word.'

'And would have kept to it,' said Owen, 'even if what he had committed himself to was not wise.'

'Very probably.' The fiki sat thinking for a moment. 'Why do you ask these things?' he said suddenly.

'I think he committed himself to something that was not wise and then found he could not go back on it.'

'You think the attack on the dam was not wise?'

'Well, no,' said Owen, startled. 'It was an attack on all. It was a blow at the common good.'

'I, on the contrary, think it was wise,' said the fiki. 'For what these new dams have brought us is not good but harm.'

'But, surely –'

122

'Harm!' repeated the fiki emphatically. 'They have brought us ill-being, not well-being. When I was young everyone in the village was strong and well. They needed to be, perhaps, because the Pashas bore down hard in those days. But they were not sick. Now they are sick from birth. The children grow up with red eyes. The men are listless in the fields. Is that good? Is that as it should be? That is what the dams have brought us. And you say that Babikr was not wise!'

'The dams have brought abundance,' said Owen.

'But at a price,' said the fiki.

'It is not the abundance that is wrong,' said Owen, 'but how it is used.'

The fiki shrugged.

'Certainly it never gets to us.'

'It is not the dams that are bad but the people.'

'You don't see the people,' said the fiki, 'but you see the dams.'

'And so you would strike at them?'

'They have destroyed a balance. In the old days there was one crop a year and the people were healthy. Now there are three and the people are sick. I would restore the balance.'

Owen was silent.

'Newness!' said the fiki. 'It is always newness! Why do we need these new dams? Were not the old good enough? Was not there water in the fields then as there is now? It is the same everywhere. They tell us this is the last year they are going to make the Cut. They are going to fill the canal in, people say, and put a tram-way on top of it. To what end? The canal brought water to the city, to us here in the Gamaliya. And now they are going to fill it in. You cannot drink tram-ways.'

'There will still be water, indeed, better water. They are building pipes – '

'Pipes!' said the old man contemptuously. 'Where once there was the canal itself, which all could see! It is not the Cut that they should be ending but all these new dams!'

'All do not think as you do,' said Owen quietly.

He got to his feet.

'I had hoped that you would help me to ease Babikr's load,'

he said, 'for I do not think that his alone was the hand that broke the dam.'

The fiki looked troubled.

'I would help Babikr if I could,' he said. 'But I do not know to whom he swore the oath.'

As Owen was going out of the door he turned back to the old man.

'Did Babikr bring you flowers?' he asked.

'Flowers?' said the fiki incredulously, looking at Owen as if he had gone out of his mind.

As Owen was crossing the Place Bab-el-Khalk, a Parquet bearer came running up to him.

'Effendi! A message. For you. Urgent!'

It was from Mahmoud. It said:

> 'Ali Khedri arrested by local police. Involved in
> fracas. Now at Gamaliya police station. Shall wait
> there for you.'

9

'I don't want to see him!' shouted Ali Khedri. 'I don't ever want to see him. Why does he come to see me?'

'He came to offer you the hand of friendship,' said Owen reprovingly.

'I spit in his hand! He kills my wife, he kills my daughter, he takes my land! And then he talks of friendship!'

'Come, this is wild talk,' said Owen. 'If he has done you injury, he wished to make amends.'

'What amends can there be after what he has done?'

'All that is in the past.'

'You have seen my house. You know how I live. Is that in the past?'

'All is not the fault of the past.'

'I tried to put the past behind me and then he sent his son!'

'What are you saying?'

'He sent his boy.'

'Suleiman?'

'Is that his name? I know the Devil has many names but did not know that was one!'

'This is wild talk. What has the boy done?'

'He took my daughter. Was it not enough to take my land? Did he have to take my daughter too?'

'If the land was taken, it is nothing to do with the boy.'

'And the boy is nothing to do with the father?'

'Not in this. The father did not know. He was afraid to tell his father. As Leila was afraid to tell you.'

'You expect me to believe that? That the Devil does not know his works?'

'This talk of the Devil is foolish. The boy's love was innocent. He did but look upon her.'

'And she looked back. Is that innocent, too?'

'She did but look.'

'And smile. Is that innocent also?'

'With a pure heart, yes. And hers was pure.'

'And talk. That, too, is innocent?'

'It was but talk. They meant nothing by it.'

'He meant something by it.'

'No more than any young boy does.'

'He knew who she was. And you still say he meant nothing by it?'

'He recognized a playmate from his childhood. That was all.'

'And he wanted to play with her again!'

'His heart was as innocent as hers. They were both as children.'

'He knew who she was and she knew who he was and you call that innocent?'

'They wished to put the past behind them. As you should, too.'

'You think he wished to put the past behind him?'

'Certainly.'

'Then why did he seek her out?'

'He did not seek her out. He saw her by chance.'

'In the whole of this big city, where no man knows another and there are a million faces, he found her by chance?'

'I think it more likely than that he should seek her out.'

'You do not know him,' said Ali Khedri with conviction. 'Nor his father.'

When Mahmoud had arrived at the water-carrier's house he had found it empty and the whole quarter in uproar. Shortly before, the police had removed Ali Khedri to the local caracol, a consequence less of his attack on Suleiman's father – the police took a relaxed view of street brawls – than of his inability to calm down. In the end, the police, exasperated, had been obliged to clip him over the head with a baton; but then, as they had explained to Mahmoud, they could not leave him lying there, 'lest his adversary return and stab him,' and so had taken him to the police station.

Indifferent to finer points of justice, they had taken Suleiman's father as well, and had been on the point of thrusting him into the cell with Ali Khedri when Mahmoud, fortunately, had arrived.

He and Owen exchanged glances. They had interrogated many times together and did not need to speak. Mahmoud took over.

'Why should he seek her out?' he asked.

'To destroy me.'

'You make too much of this,' said Mahmoud. 'It was chance that brought them together.'

'Was it chance that brought him to the Gamaliya:' demanded Ali Khedri. 'Was it by chance that he was always creeping around? Spying on me, so that I could never go out of my door without him watching?'

'He came but to gaze on your daughter. He was but a love-sick calf.'

'Oh, was that it?' said Ali Khedri, affecting surprise. 'Was that all it was? And I thought he was seeking a way to destroy me!'

'This is sick fancy!' said Mahmoud.

'Well, would that not have been enough?' whispered Ali Khedri, more to himself than to Mahmoud. 'Without the other?'

'What other?'

Ali Khedri took no notice.

'Would that not have been enough to end my hope?'

'Hope?'

'Of escape,' said Ali Khedri. 'Of life. Of not ending life like a dog.'

'Through marrying your daughter to Omar Fayoum?'

'It was there,' whispered Ali Khedri. 'There in my hand. And she took it from me.'

'She did not take it from you,' said Mahmoud. 'You took it from yourself.'

'She betrayed me.'

'She did not betray you. She sent the boy away.'

127

Ali Khedri made a gesture of dismissal.

'It was too late,' he said. 'By then the whole world knew. Omar Fayoum knew.'

'The boy wished to come to you. He wanted to ask you for her hand. He would have given you more than Omar Fayoum.'

The water-carrier smiled bitterly.

'You think so?' he said.

'He would have persuaded his father. His father loves him.'

'Loves him?' said Ali Khedri, almost as if he were encountering the words for the first time.

'His father came to you,' Mahmoud reminded him, 'seeking to make amends.'

Ali Khedri stared at him for a moment and then, very deliberately, leaned to one side and spat.

'That is what I think of his amends,' he said.

He had not injured Suleiman's father seriously. The neighbours, alarmed by the shouts, had come running and prised Ali Khedri's hands from his throat. Mahmoud asked him if he wished to press charges.

'What would be the point?' he said.

Owen and Mahmoud made a tour of the Gamaliya. The quarter was quiet now. In front of Ali Khedri's house, however, there was still a small knot of people. Mahmoud went across to them.

'Return to your houses!' he said. 'There has been enough bad work for one night.'

'What of Ali Khedri?' someone asked.

'He stays in the caracol for the night.'

'It was not his fault. Why did that man have to come pestering?'

'He came to offer the hand of friendship.'

One of the men spat derisively into the darkness. Owen thought it was Fatima's husband. He could see now that the group consisted largely of water-carriers.

'If he means friendship, why is that boy always creeping around?' said one of them.

'He is but a love-sick calf. His heart had gone to Leila.'

'Leila is dead now,' said someone, 'and he still creeps around.'

'Tell him to keep out of the Gamaliya!' called someone from the back of the group. Again Owen thought it was Fatima's husband.

'Let there be no trouble!' said Mahmoud sternly. 'Or others will find themselves joining Ali Khedri in the caracol!'

The group dispersed. Two of them crossed to Owen's side of the road. They had not seen him before. One of the men was Fatima's husband. He looked at Owen with hate in his face.

'And you, too!' he said.

'Effendi,' said Yussef, Owen's orderly, diffidently as he came into his office the next morning, 'I think you may need this.'

He put a small embroidered pouch on Owen's desk.

'What is it?'

'It is a magic charm. My wife has sewn it and inside there is a holy stone that the Sheikh has blessed.'

'Well, thank her very much – thank *you* very much, but – exactly why do I need it now?'

'If it was just the Jews, that would be nothing. They are cunning and devious, it is true, but then, you are cunning and devious also. But when you are up against this –?'

'One moment,' said Owen; 'What am I up against?'

Yussef laid his forefinger alongside his nose.

'Let us not speak the word. But, Effendi, I am with you. We are all with you. I said to my wife: "Now he is really up against it!" And she said: "Let us pray for him." And then she thought of the magic amulet. "Let us do what we can," she said; for we all want the Cut to be saved. Her especially, for, as I have said, she depends on it to have her babies.'

'That is very kind of you, Yussef. But I don't quite follow . . . Exactly what –?'

'The regulator was one thing. Bad enough – believe me, Effendi, I know what water means, my family comes from the Delta – but who would have thought it would have gone for the Cut? I said, it must be out of its mind! But the Sheikh said, no, it was not out of its mind, it was just very angry. That's because there's a lot wrong with the world, and especially with

129

the dams. We've taken things a bit too far, it's all got out of hand, and that's what it's doing, just reminding us. Well, I can understand that with the regulator, but why go for the Cut? It wouldn't have hurt it, would it, just to have held off for another week.'

'Just a minute, Yussef, who or what is "it"? Who, or what, is going for the Cut?'

'Why, Effendi, you saw for yourself. It was having a go at The Bride. The Lizard Man!'

The newspapers, too, were giving the Lizard Man a new lease of life. They were full of him. The unfortunate Babikr was quite forgotten as the link was made with the attempt on the Manufiya Regulator. One or two of the papers mentioned him as a junior accomplice or surrogate for the Lizard Man but most of the papers lost sight of him entirely, treating the incident as an unsolved mystery. Or, rather, as a mystery where one knew exactly who had perpetuated the crime but just, somehow, wasn't able to lay hands on him.

And here he was popping up again, with vaguely heroic accretions, a sort of Robin Hood perpetually thumbing his nose at the law! And, like Robin Hood, in some strange way a representative of the poor. Owen realized, as he read, that the figure was capturing popular doubt about the new dams, not so much resentment at them as worry and suspicion, the feeling that, as the fiki had said, a balance had been disturbed.

The belief that the Lizard Man had now attacked the Cut had, though, divided as well as aroused public opinion. While there were doubts about the dams, there were none about the Cut; and so with many people the 'attack' on the Cut was transformed into something positive. It did not mean, they held, that the Lizard Man was against the Cut. On the contrary, he was for it. This was just his way of registering his displeasure at the proposal to end it.

Whichever view one took, though, Owen noted with satisfaction, it had the effect of displacing the Jews from the scene. He was half minded to go down to the Muslim gravediggers and tell them that since the Lizard Man was taking a hand, they had better stay out of it!

But there was something else about the newspapers' responses that Owen found puzzling. Most of the press was strongly Nationalist, which meant that it was normally committed to a progressivist, 'modern' line. While it did not dare to turn up its nose at something as popular as the Cut, it usually tried to keep its distance from anything that smacked so strongly of backward-looking superstition. But here it was plunging heavily into popular feeling, embracing the Lizard Man for all it was worth!

What was even stranger was that it was using the situation to make a sharply critical attack on something it usually supported, the new dams and the new extensions of the irrigation system. Why were the Nationalists changing tack?

Owen went down to the Cut to see that all was well. McPhee had had the same thought and when Owen arrived was busy posting constables on top of the temporary dam and round the base of the earth cone.

'It's probably overdoing it,' he said, 'but –'

'Are you going to leave them there overnight?'

'They're not very happy at the prospect,' McPhee admitted. 'This stupid nonsense about the Lizard Man –'

McPhee was discriminating over the ritual and myth that he accepted.

Owen recognized a constable he had worked with.

'Why don't you ask Selim?'

Selim beamed when he saw Owen looking at him and waved a hand.

Owen went over to him.

'Selim, I'd like you to take charge of a few men –'

'Certainly, Effendi. These thickheads! I know how to handle them. A good kick up the backside –'

'We want to post a guard overnight and I'd like you to be in charge of it.'

'Overnight? Here?'

Selim swallowed.

'Of course, Effendi,' he said bravely.

He returned to the line, however, perturbed and thinking.

Some time later he accosted Owen.

131

'Effendi, about that guard duty –'

'Yes?'

'I would do it. In fact, I am desperate to do it. Unfortunately, there is a terrible family circumstance that pre –'

'Oh, come, Selim; there wasn't one ten minutes ago.'

'It's my grandmother, Effendi. She comes from the south, you see. Well, she can't help that. Someone has to. Only –'

'What the hell's that got to do with it?'

'But, Effendi, I was telling you! She comes from the south, you see. Down in Dinka land. Where there's nothing but reeds and not a woman in sight. Except my grandmother, of course. Well, it's very primitive down there. It's not the place where you'd want to be, believe me, Effendi. Nor me, either.'

'Selim –'

'It's very primitive down there, as I was saying. And each clan has got its totem. Would you believe it, Effendi? The backward buggers! Well, my grandmother's totem is – you'll never believe this, Effendi – a lizard! So I'm afraid that rather rules me out.'

'I don't see why.'

'Well, Effendi, it makes it doubly hard for me. I'd see him off, otherwise. What's a mere Lizard Man to a man like me? Pooh! But, you see, with it being my grandmother's totem, I'd have to beat him twice. And that, with a Lizard Man, is a bit much!'

'Well, it would be, Selim, if that were, in fact, your grandmother's totem. Only I think you may have been misinformed. You see, I know the Dinka totems; and the lizard is not among them. So you'd only have to beat him once. For a man like you . . .'

'Effendi,' said Selim, cast down, 'even a man like me could have problems with a Lizard Man!'

'I know,' said Owen, relenting, 'and therefore I will help you. It so happens that I have a magic amulet here, which, for the sake of our friendship, I am prepared to lend you.'

'Effendi!' said Selim, overjoyed. 'I will kick that Lizard Man in the balls!'

'That may not be necessary. You see, I think that if there is any problem, it will come from Muslim gravediggers –'

'Effendi, which shall I break: their backs or their necks?'

'– or the Jews.'

'Or both?'

'Just see they don't damage anything to do with the Cut, that's all.'

Selim saluted and returned, buoyant, to the line.

'Selim, you've never agreed!' Owen heard the men beside him whisper.

'What is a Lizard Man to me?' said Selim.

'But, Selim, he'll bite your ass off!'

'I'd like to see him try. Although –' he inspected his neighbour critically, 'he may bite yours off.'

'Why mine, Selim?'

'Because you're going to be with me, Abdul.'

As Owen was walking along the street a small stone landed almost at his feet. Surprised, he looked up but could see no one. He wondered for a moment if a hawk had dropped it. But it was hardly shiny enough to attract a hawk's attention. A moment later another stone skittered past him, so close that it almost hit him. He spun round but again could see no one. Children, no doubt, but all the same it was surprising.

He walked on, turned a corner and then stepped quickly back into a doorway. After a little while he heard the cautious pad of bare feet.

When the boy came round the corner he grabbed him.

'Why did you do that?'

'Ow, Effendi! Why you do this to me? I have done nothing!'

Owen held him firmly by the arm. Not by the galabeeyah – cloth could tear.

'What is your name?'

'Ali, Effendi,' the boy said sulkily.

He was about twelve years old.

'Where do you live?'

The boy made a gesture.

'There, Effendi.'

At the end of the street the broken-down houses seemed suddenly to open up. He realized that he was near the Canal.

'Which one?'

He marched the boy down the street.

'On the other side, Effendi.'

The boy pointed across the dry bed to where a derelict warehouse backed on to the Canal in a fall of rubble.

'That is not a house.'

'I don't have a house,' said the boy.

'Do you have a father or mother?'

'I don't think so.'

'So who gives you food?'

'The men do. Sometimes.'

'Did the men tell you to throw a stone at me?'

The boy was silent.

'Why do it, then?'

'You're not wanted,' said the boy. 'Here in the Gamaliya.'

On an impulse, and in some fury, Owen plunged down into the bed, dragging the boy after him. He walked across and climbed up the rubble to the warehouse. There was a cart inside and men were busy around it. They looked at him in consternation.

'If you want to throw stones at me,' raged Owen, 'don't get a boy to do it!'

'He's nothing to do with us,' one of them said after a moment.

'He'd better not be!' said Owen.

He saw now that the cart was a water-cart and recognized the driver. It was the one he'd encountered previously.

'What are you doing here?' he demanded.

'I keep my cart here,' the man said. 'Anything wrong with that?'

A man moved out of the shadow.

'Yes,' he said, 'anything wrong with that?'

Owen recognized him, too. It was Ahmed Uthman, Fatima's husband.

He went up to the two men.

'Twice,' he said, 'I have met you recently. If I have any more trouble from you, it will not be me who is not seen on the streets of the Gamaliya!'

He stood there until they yielded.

'Come on, Farag,' called one of the other men. 'Are you never going to get that horse ready?'

The driver shrugged and returned to his harnessing. After a moment, Ahmed Uthman turned, too, and walked away. As he went, he spat deliberately into the straw.

Owen knew he had to do something. His blood boiled. He went after the man and swung him round.

They stood looking at each other.

'Well?' said the water-carrier.

'I am just marking your face,' said Owen.

He let the man go, gave the other men a look, and then walked away.

He heard feet scampering behind him, stepped aside and caught the boy again.

'I was just following,' the boy protested. 'I wasn't going to throw any more stones!'

Owen released him.

'These are bad men,' he said, 'and bound for the caracol. Take care that you do not join them!'

The boy nodded.

Owen turned away. The boy fell into step behind him. Owen put his hand in his pocket and gave him a piastre. The boy saluted his thanks and dropped back.

'Tell me,' said Owen, over his shoulder; 'whose house is that?'

'Omar Fayoum's,' said the boy.

As he turned into a street he saw ahead of him the two water-carriers who had been part of the altercation with the cart driver and Ahmed Uthman the previous day.

'Hello,' he said, catching up with them. 'You, too, still walk the streets of the Gamaliya, then?'

'Yes,' said one of the men. 'But we pick our streets.'

'And we walk together,' said the other one.

Owen nodded.

'It is bad when a man has to do that,' he said. 'How long has it been like this in the Gamaliya?'

'It has been getting worse,' said one of the men, 'but it is only lately that it has got like this.'

'Why is it?' asked Owen.

The man shrugged.

'I don't know,' he said. 'Perhaps Omar Fayoum wants to fill his bag before the pipes get here.'

Further on, he met Suleiman, just coming out of a public bath-house. The boy saw him, crossed the street hurriedly, and tried to walk past.

Owen stopped him.

'Is this wise, Suleiman, to come where you have enemies?'

'I am not afraid of Ali Khedri!' said the boy fiercely.

'Perhaps not. But here in the Gamaliya Ali Khedri has friends.'

'I am not afraid of his friends, either!'

'I have met some of his friends. I think it might be wisest not to come to the Gamaliya for the next month or so.'

'I have my work to do.'

'Would you like me to speak to the Water Board? I am sure they would be willing to move you to another district.'

To his surprise, the boy shot him an angry look.

'No,' he said.

'I am concerned only for your well-being.'

The boy muttered something and tried to break away.

'Why do you not wish to be moved? It would be best, you know. Not just because of Ali Khedri's foolishness but in order to put the past behind you.'

'Everyone says, put the past behind you!' said Suleiman bitterly. 'But what if you do not want to put the past behind you?'

'She will not come back, Suleiman. Would that she could!'

The boy fidgeted and stared at the ground.

'It's not that,' he was unwillingly. 'Not just that. I know she will not come back, I *do* want to put the past behind me. But not – not just in your way. The past is what killed Leila and I want to kill it. I want to kill it here in the Gamaliya. I want to kill the ignorance and stupidity that killed Leila. And,' said Suleiman, 'I shall; by bringing my pipes.'

'It will happen. But let others do the killing.'

'No!' said Suleiman fiercely. 'I want to do it. And I want to do it not just because I want to end it – that is what Labiba says, that I must work to end the squalor and the ignorance so that there will be no more Leilas. Well, that is good, that is right. I want to do that. But I want to do more.'

'Is not that enough?'

'No. Because, you see, I know a thing that Labiba does not know. She knows that when you do something like this you make the world a better place. But I know that when you do it, you also hurt people. Well, I know who bringing the pipes will hurt. And,' said Suleiman, 'I want to hurt them.'

'Get the boy out of here!' said Owen. 'There's a gang down here and they don't like him.'

'Certainly!' said the manager at the Water Board. 'I'll see him tomorrow.' He hesitated. 'However, he may not be very willing. The fact is, I've tried to move him before. After the death of – you know about the girl?'

'Yes.'

'Well, I thought, I thought that it would be better to move him. We had a vacancy over in El Hilmiyah but he refused to go.'

'A junior effendi? Why didn't you just tell him?'

'I didn't have the heart. And besides – besides, he said he would resign. I thought that would be worse.'

'Did you think he would resign?'

'He was very adamant. But I will see him tomorrow and try again.'

'He stands a chance of getting killed if he stays in the Gamaliya.'

'I will certainly do all I can. But – what if he insists on handing in his resignation?'

Owen thought.

'He is, as you say, just a junior effendi,' the manager said. 'We would not ordinarily go to these lengths. But his father is my wife's cousin and I would like to do what I could to help him.'

'Quite so. Look, if he wants to hand in his resignation, do what you can to delay him. Tell him he's got to give notice. Meanwhile, find something else for him to do, out of the Gamaliya. There are other people who may be able to influence him. I will speak to them.'

'We don't want a killing,' said the manager. 'Bringing the

137

pipes in is difficult enough as it is. It will do them nothing but good and yet you would be surprised how many people are against them.'

'I will certainly speak to him,' promised Labiba, 'but I doubt if he will listen to me.'

'You have more influence over him than you suppose.'

'Perhaps; but I have found there are limits. I will, however, do my best. And I will also speak to Mas'udi, who has been seeing a lot of him lately. Suleiman has been helping him in his work.'

'What sort of work?'

'You are very suspicious, Captain Owen. Humble clerical duties in the evenings, mostly, I gather. Assemblymen have a great need of such help. Unpaid, that is. But I think that Suleiman has also been giving him specialized advice on water. The Nationalists are taking a great interest in water just at the moment.'

'Yes,' said Owen. 'So I have noticed.'

Owen went up to the barrage, where he found Georgiades in the Gardens lying under a tree.

'I have been walking the Gamaliya,' said Owen accusingly.

'It's been pretty hot here, too,' said Georgiades hurriedly, scrambling to his feet.

It was, indeed, hot in the Gardens that morning. As Owen had come up from the river, the heat had met him like a blow in the face. The sand was so hot that he could feel it through the soles of his shoes. When he came to the grass of the Gardens it was no cooler. The great walls of bougainvillea and datura acted like sun traps and out on the lawns the heat quivered and danced.

He made at once for the shade of the trees; along with the lemonade sellers, the peanut sellers, the Turkish delight sellers, the pastry and poultry sellers, the water-carriers and everyone else who happened to be in the Gardens at that time. They lay stretched out under the banyan and casuarina trees, every sparse item of clothing removed, including trousers. Even the birds seemed to be gasping in the heat.

'Where is it, then?' said Owen.

Reluctantly, Georgiades, not built for speed, led him through the trees towards the regulator. Ahead of them they could see the blue waters of the Nile winking in the sunlight and here and there flashes from the various water-ways enclosed behind the barrage.

They came upon the white surveyor's tapes he had seen the other day, marking out the line of the new canal. Owen was appalled to see how much of the beautiful gardens they took in.

'All this?'

Georgiades nodded, and led him in among the clumps of bougainvillea and clerodendron, already hacked back severely to allow unimpeded progress for the tapes. On the far side, the side nearest the canal, the posts holding the tapes had been torn out and the tapes broken. A loose end of tape led out towards the canal.

Just where it ended, the side of the canal had been broken. The earth had been scraped away to form a shallow trench leading down to the water, rather like the sort of place made for water-buffalo to go down to drink. Only this was too small for a water-buffalo.

The earth had been thrown back to the rear of the trench as if by the paws of some animal, and the wattles which reinforced the sides of the canal at this point, had been snapped and forced aside.

A little group of men were standing looking down at the damage. Among them were Macrae and Ferguson, and also the ghaffir and the gardener.

'It's some dog or other,' Macrae was saying. 'You'd better make inquiries in the village. And if you see it up here,' he said to the ghaffir, 'shoot it!'

The ghaffir swallowed.

'Effendi,' he said, 'it doesn't look like a dog to me.'

He touched the wattles.

'What dog could do that?'

'Well, what do you think it was, then?'

The ghaffir and the gardener looked at each other unhappily.

'The Lizard Man,' they said.

10

Standing a little way back from the canal bank was an old weeping willow. It did not provide much shade but it was the only tree hereabouts and with one accord they moved into its broken shadow. The heat rising from the bank was so great that at this time of day, just before noon, it was uncomfortable to stand there for long.

The earth had been eroded away from the foot of the willow and little lizards skittered in and out among the exposed roots. Sometimes, though, they would freeze still for a moment and then you could see the beat of their hearts under the shiny skin.

'Well,' said Macrae, 'it wasn't one of those, anyway.'

'Maybe not,' said the gardener, 'but I'll bet they're in it somewhere.'

'How could they be?'

The gardener took him by the arm.

'Be careful!' he warned. 'They'll hear you. And then they'll pass it on.'

'What I want to know,' said the ghaffir, thinking, 'is how his father managed it.'

'Managed what? Whose father?'

'The Lizard Man's father. He must have had sex with a lizard. And what I want to know is how he managed it.'

'You daft idiot!' said Macrae.

'Perhaps he was very small, Ibrahim,' suggested the gardener.

'He would have to have been.'

'Or maybe the lizard was very big?' suggested Owen.

They considered it seriously.

'That could be it,' concluded the ghaffir finally.

'For Christ's sake, man!' said Macrae, exasperated.

'Out in the desert somewhere,' suggested the ghaffir.

'It certainly wasn't in my Gardens,' said the gardener. 'We don't have them that big.'

'Yes, but out in the desert; you never know what goes on out there.'

'I can tell you one thing that doesn't go on out there,' said Ferguson, 'and that is men copulating with lizards!'

'Have you been out in the desert, Effendi? Excuse my asking.'

'Yes. Many times.'

'As far out as Siwa, Effendi?'

'Even there.'

'Perhaps it was a bit further south,' suggested the gardener. 'Darfur way. They're very primitive down there.'

'Yes. They have scorpions the size of boulders.'

'That would be it, then. If you had a lizard the size of a boulder, there'd be no problem.'

'Yes, he could have been normal size. Just like you or me.' Satisfied, the ghaffir turned to Macrae. 'Well, there you are, then, Effendi. That's how it came about.'

'Well, thanks very much. And what was it doing here, then?'

The ghaffir and the gardener looked at each other.

'The fact is, Effendi –'

'Yes?'

'The fact is, it doesn't like what is going on,' said the ghaffir.

'It doesn't like this idea of building a canal right across the Gardens,' said the Gardener.

'Oh, you think so? And perhaps it didn't like the regulator providing water for the Gardens either? Not to mention the Delta?'

'I think, Effendi,' said the gardener hesitantly, 'I think it's quite liked the dams up till now. But now it's going off them. It thinks we're taking things a bit too far.'

'Which is about the one sensible thing they said,' said Owen afterwards.

'Taking it too far? Man, have you not read the reports?'

'Er, no. Not in detail, that is. No, not in detail. But I think it's true that popular feeling is turning against the dams.'

'You're wrong there,' said Macrae positively. 'This is a country in which everyone knows the value of water. Every man jack of them! You're surely not taking seriously –?'

'The Lizard Man? No. That's just something the popular imagination has conjured up. But it conjured it up precisely because it needs something to express the uneasiness it feels about the dams.'

'And you think that the attack on the regulator was something to do with this?'

'I think,' said Owen, 'that it's becoming very important to find out who the people behind Babikr are.'

Coming away, to his surprise he met Suleiman's father. He was standing beneath a casuarina tree looking at the regulator. He smiled when he saw Owen and walked out to meet him.

'I thought I would have a look at it while I was here,' he said.

'The regulator?'

'Yes. It's the one that feeds water down into the Delta, you know. It's very important to me. My lands depend on it.'

'So you've been hit, then, by this attack?'

'Yes. To a certain extent. It would have been more if it had not been for Macrae Effendi's prompt actions.'

'You, presumably, are one of many.'

'Oh, yes. But I am more directly affected than most because my lands lie beside the Canal itself. The others get their water mostly from feeders.'

'Will it make a big difference to you?'

'Not very. You see, we were all ready for it. The gates were going to be opened the following week and we had made our preparations. So when we heard the surge was coming, all we had to do, really, was open our own gates. Of course, there was a lot of extra flooding but in a way I don't mind that. Water is water. We're glad to see it whenever it comes.'

'It didn't do much damage, then?'

'It did some, and would have done more if we hadn't been able to take steps in time. What saved us was the telephone. These modern inventions, Effendi! Say what you like, but they do make a difference! I had recently had one put in, the only farm to do so, I think, in the province, and how glad I am now that I did! But, you see, again it was Macrae Effendi – he had his man phoning all the way down the system to let them know what was coming. The wonders of the modern world are great, Effendi, but without the wonders of modern men they would be nothing!'

Over among the trees there was suddenly some movement.

'Ah,' said Suleiman's father, 'that will be Mas'udi.'

'The Assemblyman?'

'Yes. He is our district's representative. We had arranged to meet here.'

It was indeed Mas'udi, in a heavy dark suit, just the wrong thing for the Gardens on a day like this, and the usual tarboosh of the prosperous effendi. He was mopping his face with a large silk handkerchief.

'Hannam!'

'Mas'udi!'

The two men embraced.

'You know the Mamur Zapt, of course?'

Mas'udi looked at him curiously.

'Of course. But I did not expect to meet him here.'

'We met by chance,' said Owen. 'I have just been visiting the regulator.'

'We, too,' said Mas'udi, 'are visiting the regulator.'

'Ah, yes. Mr Hannam was telling me. The land will be, of course, in your district.'

'Yes. A matter of immediate and very great concern to me. And to my constituents.'

'It certainly is,' said Suleiman's father.

'I thought I would bring Al-Sayyid Hannam here and show him how things stood. Then he can go home and tell them that at least something has been done.'

'Thanks to you, Mas'udi,' said Suleiman's father.

'Well,' said Mas'udi modestly, 'not just to me. But I have indeed been pressing.'

'But I thought,' said Owen maliciously, 'from what you were saying in the Assembly the other day, Mr Mas'udi, that you had reservations?'

'I do, I do. But not over replacing the regulator. That must be done at once. Over the cost!'

Suleiman's father nodded approvingly.

'Taxpayers' money, Captain Owen! We must be vigilant!'

'I thought, however, from what you said, that –'

'Reservations? About replacing the regulator? Oh dear, no!' Mas'udi shook his head vigorously. 'Those of us who live in the Delta know only too well the significance of such things!'

'Nevertheless, I had the impression that you and your colleagues were changing your ground with respect to the Government's irrigation proposals?'

'If so, then we are changing with public opinion. To which, unfortunately, the Government remains indifferent!'

He cast a quick glance at Suleiman's father. Mr Hannam's face, however, remained impassive.

'In any case we are not against maintaining a basic infrastructure. The Manufiya Regulator must, of course, be replaced. I shall insist on that. It is only rash and foolish endeavours that we question. And then, of course, it is true that other questions were asked. About health, for instance –'

'There's always been bilharzia in the Delta,' said Suleiman's father.

'Exactly. And it's time something was done about it.'

'I don't know that anything can –'

'Modern methods, Mr Hannam. Such as your son is using in a different, though related, sphere.'

'Suleiman?'

'A great help to me, Mr Hannam! An invaluable source of advice!'

'He is?' said Suleiman's father, pleased.

'I don't mind saying to you, Mr Hannam, what I have said to so many others: that boy, I said, is this country's future!'

144

'He's certainly come on a lot –'

Mas'udi led them out onto the regulator embankment and began to explain, rather knowledgably, Owen thought, the extent of the damage to the gates.

Suleiman's father, evidently not ignorant himself, stepped across to the other side and then began to walk along the opposite bank to get a better view.

Owen seized the opportunity to have a word with Mas'udi.

'Have you had a chance to speak to the boy yet?'

'Speak to the boy?'

'I thought that Labiba Latifa was going to –?'

'Oh yes. She did mention it to me. It was to do with a move, wasn't it? I think the boy is quite happy where he is.'

'That's not the point. His life may be in danger. There's a gang –'

'Gang?' said Mas'udi. 'Life in danger? Surely you're the one to see about that!'

Some workmen had caught a chameleon. They had cleared a space for it on the canal bank, scuffing back the sand to make little surrounding walls and to leave the space inside as an arena. Into the space, along with the chameleon, they had put a grasshopper and were now crowding round to watch the contest.

It was, clearly, going to be an unequal one. The grasshopper could do nothing to the chameleon but the chameleon could do plenty to the grasshopper. The issue was simply how long the grasshopper would survive.

Its chances, however, were not negligible. The chameleon would shoot out its four to five inches of tongue to lasso its prey; but if the grasshopper turned its jumps adroitly enough, it could make the chameleon miss; and if it could go on doing this long enough the chameleon's tongue muscles would tire, it would stop shooting and the grasshopper would be declared the winner.

The contest was just beginning as Owen walked past and already, apparently, the grasshopper had done enough to attract some sizeable bets. Owen could see the coins set out in a dirty handkerchief.

One of the workmen touched his arm as he went past.

'He's been here before,' he said, jerking his head in the direction of Mas'udi and Al-Sayyid Hannam.

'Which one?'

'The effendi.'

Mas'udi. Owen nodded.

'How long ago?'

'Before the regulator went.'

Owen nodded again and slipped his hand in his pocket.

'Did he talk to anyone?'

'He had someone with him.'

'Who?'

'A boy. An effendi.'

Owen jingled the coins in his pocket.

'Did they talk to anyone else?'

'I don't think so.'

'Babikr?'

'I don't think so.'

Owen brought his hand out.

'What did they do, then?'

'They just looked.'

'At the regulator?'

'At the regulator.'

Owen dropped some coins into the man's hand; which went on the chameleon.

He took a felucca back to the city. At this time of day there were not many passengers, only a small group of fellahin who squatted on the deck with a hamper of chickens and chatted animatedly, and a donkey loaded up with berseem, clover for the cab horses of the city. Owen sat at the back on the raised steering platform, where the master sprawled with his hand on the tiller.

On the Nile the prevailing wind is from the north while the current is from the south, a happy state of affairs which means that, with a little bit of luck, in either direction the crew has very little to do. Today the wind was just strong enough to offset the current and the felucca moved slowly upstream.

Out on the river there was no protection from the sun and

the glare from the water was hard on the eyes. Owen usually didn't bother about sunglasses but today he wished that he had brought them.

The steersman reached over the side and splashed water over his head. He asked Owen if he would like a drink. When Owen said he would, he dipped an empty beer bottle into the river, pulled it up and gave it to him.

'Try this,' he said. 'You won't get water like this in Cairo!'

One of the fellahin looked up.

'That's right,' he said. 'You know what they always say? The best water comes from the middle of the river!'

He stretched out his hand for the bottle after Owen.

'And the thing is,' said the steersman, 'it's free.'

'It's free out here,' said the fellah, 'but it soon won't be in the city.'

'What's that?'

'They say the only way you'll be able to get water in future will be through pipes. And it stands to reason you're not going to get that for nothing.'

The steersman shrugged.

'The river will still be there, won't it? And there will still be water-carriers.'

'Ah, but will there?' said the fellah.

On an impulse Owen decided not to get off the boat at Bulak but to go on to the stop opposite Roda Island, where he would be able to see how preparations for the Cut were proceeding.

Already the entrance to the Canal was jammed with boats. There was hardly enough room for the Kadi's barge to get through. Owen could see it across the river, moored off Roda Island. Workmen were busy putting the finishing touches to its finery. Lanterns hung from the rigging, the ornamental chairs were already in position, and there, on a raised platform in the bows, were the cannon.

Both banks of the Canal were now a mass of stalls. There seemed hardly room for the spectators. Already, though, some forward souls were camping out, reserving their positions.

Down in the canal bed little boys milled about, making a

147

game of trying to break through the police cordon around the cone and climb to the top. Occasionally one or two nearly succeeded, only to be retrieved by chiding constables. Everything seemed very good-humoured.

He caught sight of Selim on the other side of the cone, chatting to some heavily hennaed peanut sellers who were cackling loudly at his jokes. He abandoned them when he saw Owen and came across to him.

'Effendi,' he said, 'they have been here.'

'Who?'

'The gravediggers. They said they wanted to look the dam over. It was in case the Jews dropped out.'

'Did you let them?'

'Yes, but I didn't let them get too close. I said – you'll like this, Effendi, it's a good one – I said, "my boss will bite your ass". And they said: "Oh, yes; and who's your boss, then?" And I said – this is it, Effendi – I said: "It's the Lizard Man!" And they said: "What the hell's he got to do with it?" And I said: "He's been doing what you've just been doing: looking the job over." Well, they didn't like the sound of that. And then they asked, how did I know? And I said: "He was sniffing around the other night and left his mark." And they didn't like the sound of that, either. "So, my little petals," I said, "you'd better watch your butts if he's taking an interest in proceedings this time!" And they spoke big, and said he wasn't the only one who was taking an interest in proceedings this time, and they weren't the ones who needed to watch out. But, Effendi, I could see that they were worried. And, besides, Effendi, the biggest of them is but a flea compared with me.'

'Suppose,' said Zeinab, 'she *had* died as a consequence of the circumcision: what would you have done then?'

Mahmoud shifted in his chair uneasily.

'The issue doesn't arise,' he said.

'But it must arise all the time,' objected Zeinab. 'Circumcision of women is common in the poor quarters; and in those conditions it must often go wrong.'

'The practice is not against the law,' said Mahmoud.

'So you would do nothing?'

'I would look at the circumstances,' said Mahmoud, 'to see if a legal issue arose.'

'Ah, so it could arise?'

Owen could see that Mahmoud was in for a hard time of it. He had arranged the meeting at Zeinab's request. Women did not ask for meetings with men and Mahmoud would have been paralysed if she had. He found talking to Zeinab difficult enough as it was. Not only was she a woman, she was the daughter of a Pasha; and not only was she the daughter of a Pasha, she was the daughter of a particularly free-thinking one, brought up to converse with a freedom that Mahmoud found shocking.

This business of circumcision, for instance, was something a woman should never discuss with a man, not unless he was her husband. True, Owen was here, but then he wasn't, strictly speaking, Zeinab's husband. Tormented, he cast a despairing look at Owen.

'Presumably, there could be issues of negligence,' said Owen.

Mahmoud seized on this with relief. On female circumcision he could think of nothing he could with propriety say; on legal issues he could talk forever. He launched into a highly technical, safely logical explanation.

'You surely don't expect a woman in the Gamaliya to understand all this?' said Zeinab.

'Well, no. She would have to consult a lawyer.'

'You, for instance.'

'Well –'

The thought filled him with panic. On other occasions Zeinab would have enjoyed tormenting him. Today, however, she was concentrating on the law, not the lawyer.

'I think trying to find a remedy that way is no good,' she said. 'It's too complicated. It's the practice itself that's got to be attacked.'

There was a little silence.

'I think I'm coming to agree with you,' said Mahmoud, surprisingly.

'You are?'

Zeinab looked at him with favour.

'The trouble is,' said Mahmoud, with a slight shrug. 'I don't see how it is to be done.'

'Education,' said Owen, 'of women.'

'Men,' said Zeinab.

'Legislation would, of course, be the answer,' said Mahmoud. He looked at Zeinab. 'Perhaps your father –?'

'Suicide,' said Zeinab firmly. 'Political suicide. That's how he would see it. In any case, it's no good hoping for anything from the old guard. But perhaps the Nationalists –?'

She looked at Mahmoud.

'Not on a thing like this,' said Mahmoud unhappily. 'Not yet, at any rate.'

They both looked at Owen.

'The Government?'

'I don't think the Khedive –'

'The British,' said Zeinab, whose knowledge of the political situation, though sketchy, was realistic.

'I don't think we would interfere with local practice on a thing like this,' said Owen.

'You interfere with the women,' said Zeinab nastily.

'But,' said Mahmoud, 'it wasn't circumcision, it was garotting.'

He and Owen were lingering over their coffee, Zeinab had departed for art galleries unknown, and Mahmoud was bringing Owen up to date with where he had got to on the Leila killing.

The key information from his point of view was that, according to the stall-holder's wife, Leila had left the *souk* with a man who appeared to be known to her. Now there were not many men she could have known, or should have known, added Mahmoud primly. It was the other side of the seclusion of Islamic women.

'They are not all like Zeinab,' said Mahmoud, getting, perhaps, his own back.

Leila came from a poor household and did the shopping herself so she was known to such people as the stall-holders in the *souk*, although that did not mean that they had ever seen her face. Figure, they knew, and voice, and some of their wives had been to her house where they might have

150

seen her unveiled; and some of the older people remembered seeing her face when she was a little girl and played with the children on the rubble heaps among the derelict houses.

'She had a sweet nature,' they said.

And that was the general opinion of the quarter. Timid and retiring she might have been, invisible she might have thought herself behind the long black veil, but everyone seemed to have known her. And the one thing they were all agreed on was that she was certainly not a loose woman.

'Her?' scoffed one of the women. 'She was that proper she never even looked at a man.'

And yet she had been seen with one, appeared to have gone off with one.

'Well, if she did, you can be sure there was nothing wrong with it!' declared a woman, one of a group assembled by Um Fattouha.

'She went with the boy,' Mahmoud had pointed out.

Smiles all round. Apparently that did not count. The Gamaliya ladies were romantics at heart.

'They were like babes!' they said.

'I doubt if they ever got as far as holding hands.'

'You all knew about it?' said Mahmoud, surprised.

'We weren't born yesterday!'

'You could see it in his face!'

'They used to wait for each other.'

'She was that put out one day when he didn't come. And then when he arrived all huffing and puffing, she wouldn't have anything to do with him. Made him walk behind her.'

Which was not the way it usually was.

'Ah, but then she felt sorry for him, didn't she?'

'Within about two yards!'

They all burst out laughing. And they dismissed out of hand any possibility that Suleiman could have been the attacker.

'It's not in him!'

Mahmoud was not so sure.

Or, at any rate, he was not ruling it out. Because if it was not Suleiman, who else could it have been?

'However unlikely,' he said, 'you have to look at all the men she knew.'

And so he had come to her father.

First, though, he had scrupulously checked for others. Had she uncles? Cousins?

'Not up here,' they said. 'Back in the village, maybe. But they never come up here.'

'Sometimes they do,' someone objected, 'I remember a cousin once.'

'Ah, but he was up here to do his corvée. He didn't come up to see them especially.'

Men from the village did drop in from time to time if they happened to be in Cairo. Usually it was when they came up to do their annual duties maintaining the Nile banks and dams. It wasn't usually the same person, however, just whoever happened to be up that year from the village, bringing the villagers' greetings and a few presents.

'There were no regular visitors?'

Not that they remembered.

Friends? What about other friends?

'Friends?' said one of the women. 'That old bastard never had any!'

'I'm not so sure about that,' said Owen, sipping his coffee. 'What about Fatima's husband? He and Ali Khedri seem to hang around together.'

'I asked about him,' said Mahmoud. 'Fatima said that in fact they weren't very close.'

'Close enough for them to take Leila in when her father threw her out,' said Owen.

'That was her doing, not his. She had known Leila since she was a child. But the two men hadn't been very close. It was only in the past year that they'd been getting together. She rather agreed with the others: Ali Khedri didn't have friends.'

'Not even among the water-carriers?'

'Apparently not.'

'They're a tight-knit group over in the Gamaliya,' said Owen.

'Yes, but the others don't like him. They say he's too bitter.'

'A surly devil,' one of the women had called him.

'He was better before his wife died.'

'She was a saint; and Leila took after her.'

'Never a cross word!'

'He could have done with a few. Particularly after his wife died. The way he treated that girl!'

'Yes, but he treated everyone like that.'

'It got so that people didn't like going to his house.'

'What about when people did go to his house?' asked Mahmoud. 'Did they see Leila?'

'They wouldn't have done. He was very strict. He always used to send her out. They only had the one room so she used to have to go out into the yard.'

'There was no one, then, who might have had his eye on her?'

'They didn't get the chance.'

'Omar Fayoum?'

The women looked at each other.

'I don't know how he came to light on her. Maybe he'd seen her about in the streets. Bringing her father's food. I'll bet he liked that! Thought that was the kind of girl he wanted!'

Patiently Mahmoud had worked through all the men she might have known. And in the end he was left with the father.

'He had just quarrelled with her,' Mahmoud pointed out. 'Badly enough to throw her out of his house. He had built a lot on her. And then it had all collapsed. He blamed her.'

'Well, yes, but –'

'I know. But most murders occur within the family. And this wasn't a particularly good family. Anyway, I checked his movements that night. Fatima had gone to see him when Leila had not come back, and she had found him in. We know that because there are independent witnesses. They heard them quarrelling. But that was probably after the assault. What about earlier in the evening?'

Mahmoud had asked Ali Khedri that.

'What business is it of yours?' Ali Khedri had said truculently.

Mahmoud had told him.

Grudgingly Ali Khedri had told him that he had finished his

153

water-carrying rounds early that day and gone to help Omar Fayoum's driver to unharness the horse. They had stayed for a while, chatting.

'How long?' asked Mahmoud.

'How do I know?'

About a couple of hours, he had finally acknowledged.

'Who was there?'

Omar Fayoum, the cart driver, Ahmed Uthman and one or two others.

When had he left?

When it began to get dark; which would have put it at just about the time that Leila was setting out for the *souk*.

'Did you leave with anyone?'

Ahmed Uthman; but then they had parted, Ahmed to his house, Ali Khedri to his.

'Ahmed Uthman confirms that,' said Mahmoud. 'But what of course we don't know is what happened after they separated.'

According to Ali Khedri, he had stayed at home. He had made himself some supper. He had not gone out. No one had called; until that silly bitch Fatima had burst in with all her shouting.

'I've had people out checking if anyone saw him that night,' said Mahmoud. 'So far without success.'

'Why are you asking me these questions?' Ali Khedri had shouted in the end.

'You attacked one,' Mahmoud had said. 'Might you not have attacked another?'

'My own daughter?'

'From the way you have spoken of her,' said Mahmoud, 'yes.'

'It's not me you want to be talking to,' Ali Khedri had shouted. 'It's that boy!'

11

It was the last time – or so everyone present hoped – that they would have to meet, the last occasion, as McPhee, with a sense of history, pointed out, on which there would actually be a meeting of the Cut Committee.

'When will they start filling in the canal?' asked the Kadi.

'Oh, not for some months yet,' said the Minister. 'We're still not quite sure of the money.'

'Surely some has been set aside?' said Paul.

'Yes, but there's talk of raiding it. To pay for the new Manufiya Regulator, you know.'

'Is there any chance of the whole thing being put off?' asked the Kadi. 'At least for another year? That would be very popular.'

'I doubt it,' said the Minister. 'The contracts have been let.'

They had reviewed the arrangements for the day. It would start early. During the night the workmen would have been busy cutting away the dam until only the thickness of a foot was left. At sunrise the Kadi's barge would appear and the Kadi would read a proclamation.

'The usual turgid stuff, I'm afraid,' said the Kadi.

Then a boat would be pushed through the remaining earth wall.

'Not mine, I hope?' said the Kadi anxiously.

'No, a small one,' said McPhee, 'with an officer inside it.'

'Stout fellow!' murmured the Kadi, relieved.

'Then the water will pour through and demolish "The Bride".'

'That will be all right, will it? I mean, it will be demolished?'

'Oh yes.'

'We wouldn't want anything to go wrong. The Bride's been a bit unfortunate this year.'

'Look,' said McPhee, 'they've been doing this for nearly two thousand years.'

'Just making sure.'

'What about the gold?' said McPhee.

'Gold?'

'They used to distribute purses of gold among the crowd.'

'Well, they're not going to this time!' said Paul. 'The treasury would have a fit.'

'What about policing?' asked Garvin.

'All ready, sir,' said McPhee. 'I've got extra men out this time. In view of – well, you know.'

'What about that?' asked Paul. 'Where have we got to over who is going to do the actual Cut?'

'Still dangling. The Jews are still making up their minds about whether they're prepared to do it but for no extra money. And the Muslim gravediggers are still hoping they'll say no.'

'Well, they'll have to make up their minds tomorrow evening.'

'That's when we can expect trouble,' said Owen.

'We'll be ready for them,' promised McPhee, grim-faced, however.

'Actually, I've got a suggestion,' said Owen.

'So long as it doesn't cost money,' said the Minister.

'Well, it needn't cost any extra money. It's more a question of cost displacement.'

'My God!' said Paul. 'He's talking like an accountant! And I thought he was a friend of mine!'

'It was your saying that they might raid the money to pay for the regulator that gave me the idea,' said Owen, turning to the Minister.

'Look,' said the Minister, 'one raid is enough!'

'No, no. That wasn't the idea. The thing is, the Canal is going to have to be filled in. And they're going to have to pay people to do that. Well, why shouldn't we promise that work to the Jews and the gravediggers? On condition that they don't cause trouble tomorrow? The work will have to be done by someone, won't it?'

'I quite like this idea,' said Paul.

'It would get us off the hook,' said Garvin.

'Wouldn't it be merely postponing trouble?' asked the Kadi. 'I mean, they're still going to find it difficult to work together.'

'They wouldn't need to work together,' said Owen. 'The Jews could start at one end, the Muslim gravediggers from the other.'

'I think this is a brilliant idea!' cried the Kadi. 'We could make it a race!'

'First to get there gets a bonus, you mean?' asked the Minister.

'I was thinking of honour and personal satisfaction,' said the Kadi reprovingly.

'I was thinking that if they got to the middle at different times, they need never actually meet,' said Owen. 'And then there would be no trouble.'

'You know,' said Paul, 'this suggestion has considerable merit.'

'It is a suggestion,' said the Kadi, admiring, 'worthy of the Mamur Zapt.'

'Right, then,' said Paul briskly. 'That settled? Anything else?'

'Well, there's the Lizard Man,' said the Kadi.

'Yes,' said the Minister. 'There's the Lizard Man.'

'Lizard Man?' said Paul.

'Active around "The Bride of the Nile", apparently.'

'I've got a guard on,' said McPhee.

'Against the Lizard Man?' said Paul.

'I hope there's going to be no diversion of resources away from the dams,' said the Minister. 'Guards are needed there, too, you know.'

'I thought the chap was in prison?'

'No, no. Against the Lizard Man.'

'Just a minute,' said Paul, pulling himself together; 'we've got guards everywhere against the Lizard Man?'

'At the Cut, certainly.'

'Exactly why – would you tell me exactly why – it has

been found necessary to have guards against – against a – a Lizard Man?'

'There have been rumours that he's taking an interest in the Cut this year.'

'It's not the Cut I'm bothered about,' said the Minister. 'It's the dams. We've got a lot of money tied up there, you know. If another went – '

'I think the Cut is the more immediate danger,' said the Kadi.

'What makes you think a threat is posed to – to either the Cut or the dams by – by – by a Lizard Man?'

'There have been incidents,' said the Kadi.

'Have there?' Paul was looking at Owen.

'Sort of.'

'He's blown one up,' said the Minister. 'He could blow up another.'

'But I thought –?' ?'

'I doubt if the incidents themselves amount to anything,' said Owen. 'The point is, though, that the public thinks they do.'

'I see. And you hope that when it sees a guard, it will feel reassured?'

'I hope so. Actually,' said Owen, 'it's a bit more complicated than that. As I say, I don't think the incidents themselves amount to anything, but it's what, in a way, they express that is important.'

'And what is that?'

'Anti-Government feeling,' said the Kadi.

'Anti-British feeling,' the Minister corrected him hurriedly.

'You think the Lizard Man is a Nationalist?' asked Paul.

'Well, no,' admitted the Minister. 'It's just that there's a lot of popular unrest at the moment over the ending of the Cut and they blame –'

'There's a lot of feeling, too, about the dams,' said the Kadi.

'Well,' said Paul, beginning to gather up his papers, 'I don't know that there's a lot this Committee can do about either of those. As for the Lizard Man,' – he took care not to meet Owen's eye – 'that, I feel, is the sort of thing that is best left to the Mamur Zapt.'

*   *   *

When Owen got back to the Bab-el-Khalk he found his orderly, Yussef, fussing around in his office, changing, among other things, the water in the earthenware pitcher which, as in all Cairo offices, stood in the latticed window. The theory was that the breeze would cool it but that, of course, worked only when there was a breeze. Today there wasn't and the water was on the hot side of lukewarm. It had, moreover, a fly in it, which Yussef dispatched, with the water, out of the window. Then he refilled the pitcher from the big brass-beaked jug that he was carrying.

'It's the best, Effendi,' he said reassuringly to Owen. 'Straight from the river.'

'Oh, good.' Owen took a sip.

He put the glass down.

'Straight from the river, you say?'

He had only just begun to think about such things.

'It's all right, Effendi,' said Yussef anxiously. 'It's not green.'

'Green' water was the first of the year's 'new' water, the beginnings of the new flood, so-called because of the greenish tinge given it by either the vegetable matter of the Sudd or the algae of the Sobat (opinion was divided). Opinion was divided again over the properties of the 'green' water. Did it induce love-sickness? Or did it merely cause diarrhoea?

Green or not, the water was the only water in town, or, at least, in the Bab-el-Khalk and Owen had been happily drinking it for the past two or three years. Now, however, he sipped it meditatively.

'Effendi,' said Yussef, eager, possibly, to divert him, 'there is a man to see you.'

'There is?' Owen put the glass down. 'How long has he been waiting?' he demanded.

Yussef waved the question aside.

'He is but a fellah, Effendi,' said Yussef dismissively. Yussef had been but a fellah too but now that he had risen to the dizzy heights of orderly he was inclined to look down upon his country cousins.

'Show him in!'

Suleiman's father came diffidently into the room.

'Effendi –'

'Mr Hannam!'

And to show Yussef what ought to be what, Owen ordered coffee.

'Effendi, I apologize for disturbing you when you must be so busy but Labiba Latifa told me –'

'Labiba Latifa? You've met her?'

'Yes, and she told me that you were concerned about – Effendi, I have tried to persuade him, I have even used a father's authority, although that doesn't seem to go far these days –'

'What about?'

'My son. You asked Labiba –'

'Yes, indeed. I advised her to use her influence to get the boy out of the Gamaliya for a time. And you have been adding your efforts?'

'Well, yes, Effendi. But without success. He will not listen to me. He will not listen to his father! He says he is on the brink of finding out something that his chiefs will be very pleased about and that will make his career. He asks me if I do not wish well for him, if that is not what I want, him to do well, to make a success of his career? And, Effendi, I do, that is what I sent him up here for. Water is our life-blood, I told him, but it comes in different forms. In the fields it is sweat, in the city it is money. Effendi, I have laboured in the fields and done well enough, but that is not what I want for my boy. And now he says: "Father, I have done what you ask and now, just when I am getting somewhere, you bid me to leave!" "You can do as well elsewhere," I said. But he said: "No, father. We get but one chance in our life – you have told me that yourself – and for me this is it!" So what shall I do, Effendi? What shall I say to him? I come to you!'

'Has he said what he is on the brink of finding out?'

'No, Effendi. It is to do with his work.'

'I think I know what it is. It is important but it is nothing compared with his life.'

'You think it may come to that?' said Suleiman's father, troubled.

'I hope not. Nevertheless, he has enemies in the Gamaliya. As you have.'

'He is too young to have enemies. Such enemies!'

'I think so, too. And therefore I think he would be better out of the Gamaliya.'

'I begin to wish I had never sent him up here. Terrible things happen in the city. First that girl. Then this!'

'Good things happen also, and they can happen to him. But I think it would be well if he were out of the Gamaliya for a time. He stands on the brink, you say? How near is that? Is it a matter of days? Or weeks?'

'I do not know. Days, I think.'

'If it were a day or two, and if he watched his step, all could yet be well.'

'I will tell him that,' said Suleiman's father, relieved.

'But let it not drag on!' Owen warned.

'I will tell him that, too. And insist that a father's authority shall not be set aside!'

Yussef brought coffee. Over its aromas, Suleiman's father calmed down.

'What things happen in the city, Effendi!' he sighed. 'What things happen in the city!'

'Things happen in the country, too,' said Owen, 'and one thing that especially interests me is what happened once, years ago, between Ali Khedri and yourself.'

Suleiman's father was silent for a while, a long while. Owen sipped his coffee and waited. He knew better than to hurry the old man. In Egypt, where all present things had roots in the past, such conversations took a long time.

'It was a dispute over water,' said Suleiman's father at last. 'In the villages most disputes are. We ploughed adjoining fields. Between our fields there was an old canal, not much used because now there was a new and better one which went past the end of my field but not past his. I allowed him to build a gadwal across my land and take off water from the new canal. The old canal was on my land and one day I decided to fill it in. Ali Khedri objected.

"You cannot do that," he said.

"Look," I said, "we have the new canal and I have allowed

you water. The old canal stands idle, and it is on my land. I will plant it with cotton."

'But Ali Khedri said:

'"The canal is not yours but the village's."

'I said:

"It is on my land."

'Well, we went to the sheikh and to the omda and then to the Inspector and they said that I was in the right. So I filled it in and planted cotton. And Ali Khedri was very angry and one night he came and beat the cotton down. And I said: "If that is what you do, then I will beat you down!" And I tore out his gadwal.'

'So then he was without water?'

'He had to carry it. Well, it is hard to carry enough if you have fields, and his crops dwindled and my crops throve. I would have let him build his gadwal again if he had said a soft word, but he did not. So I hardened my heart against him.'

'Did not the neighbours bring you together?'

'They tried but he would not listen to them. "I would rather carry," he said, "than accept from him, even though I go poor." Well, he went poor and in the end he had to leave, and now I own his fields, and many others.'

He looked at Owen.

'These things are not good, I know, but life in the fields is hard. Although not as hard as life in the city if you are a water-carrier.'

In this heat you needed to take fluid frequently and some time later Owen found himself pouring out another glass of water. As he raised it to his lips his conversation with Yussef came back into his mind. He put the glass down again.

'Yussef,' he said, 'where does this water come from?'

'The river, Effendi. Right from the middle. It's the best.'

'But how did it get here? Here, to the Bab-el-Khalk?'

Yussef shifted his turban to the back of his head and scratched.

'How did it get here? In a water-cart, I suppose.'

* * *

'Water-cart?' said the man from the Water Board indignantly. 'No it doesn't! You're one of the buildings on the pipes!'

'I've never seen them.'

'Well, you wouldn't, would you? They're underground. Look, there are two sorts of pipes and they bring two sorts of water.'

'From the river?'

'From our pumping station on the river. One sort of water is filtered and that's for drinking. That's the stuff, I hope, that Yussef gives you. The other sort is unfiltered – it comes straight out of the river – and that is for irrigation. It's the sort of stuff you see in the parks and gardens on watering days. We turn the cocks on and flood the place. And then it all seeps down into the ground and comes back again, into the river. Water-carts? Look, water-carts are a health hazard, about as big a danger to health as that bloody old canal they're about to fill in. It's all right when they're carrying water to damp down the dust in the streets but what some of the buggers do is sell water from the cart for drinking. And that's not the worst of it!'

'No?'

'No. They even tap our pipes – the ones we use to carry water for irrigation in – and sell *that* for drinking!'

'Did I hear someone say the magic word?' said Macrae, coming towards them with a bottle.

'Water?'

'No. Drinking.'

He poured them both a generous dram. It was the rehearsal for Burns Night that Macrae had invited him to. Scotsmen were there in abundance. So, too, were many whom Owen had hitherto never suspected to be Scottish. Paul, for example.

'Mother's side,' he claimed.

He was talking to the man from the Khedive's Office.

'But, just a minute,' the man was saying, 'there he is!'

They looked across the room and saw the pink young man who had been responsible for despoiling the Khedive's Summer Palace.

'I thought he was in the Glass House?' said the man from the Khedive's Office. 'Being tortured?'

'Oh, he is, he is!' Paul assured him. 'He's just been let out for this special occasion.'

'He doesn't look as if he is being tortured,' said the Khedive's man.

'I should hope not!' said Paul indignantly. 'We British are trained to keep a stiff upper lip!'

'Even so –'

'Besides,' said Paul, 'the whole point is that it should be lingering.'

'Perhaps you are starting too gently?' suggested the man from the Khedive's Office.

'You think so?' Paul inspected the pink man critically. 'Of course, it would be underneath his kilt,' he said.

'You mean – ?'

Paul nodded.

'Well, that's the place to start,' said the Khedive's man, impressed. 'The genitals.'

'He bears it well, don't you think?' said Paul.

'Well, he does. And yes, perhaps you're right. You don't want them to die too quickly. It's a fine judgement. Well, I'm sure the British know what they're doing.'

Cairns-Grant was there, also kilted. Owen asked him if he carried a surgical knife in his stocking instead of a skean dhu.

'Nae,' said Cairns-Grant. 'I keep a wee bottle of Islay there. In case the other runs out.'

'Now, look,' said Owen, 'have you been talking to the Nationalists lately?'

'Are you accusing me of being subversive?'

'I'm just wondering where all these ideas on health are coming from.'

'Well. They're not all coming from me, I can tell you. That lassie, Labiba –'

'On circumcision, I grant you.'

'Well, she's got something there. In the case of pharaonic circumcision – you know, where all the girl's genital organs are excised – we estimate that complications occur in over fifty per cent of the cases. And where they occur we estimate that death results in over fifty per cent of cases.'

'Okay, she's beginning to persuade me. Not that I can do much about it.'

'Ah, well, there you are, you see. That's what we all say. And it's true, you see, not just of circumcision but of a lot of other mortality too. And not just mortality, disease. A lot of it could be avoided. That's why I've been talking to the Nationalists.'

'And that applies to water-borne illnesses, too?'

'It does,' Cairns-Grant looked across the room to where Macrae and Ferguson, bottles in hand, were welcoming new arrivals. 'Now you see those two laddies; if anyone told them that what they were doing was not for the benefit of the public, they'd laugh at you. And a lot of what they do does benefit the public. Egypt would be a great deal worse than it is if it weren't for them. They're grand laddies. But I'm beginning to wonder if they've not got it wrong.'

Macrae came bustling across.

'Are you talking to that auld resurrectionist?' he said to Owen. 'I'll bet he's touting for business again. "Bring me the bodies, Owen! As long as you keep them coming, I'm all right for a job!"'

Cairns-Grant threw back his head and laughed.

'Well,' he said, 'there's no doubt I'm in the right place. Egypt's a great country – for pathologists.'

Later in the evening the reeling began. The dancing, that is. Owen reeled too; and as the evening wore on and the supply of whisky continued, he reeled more and more.

At one point he was sure he could hear Cairns-Grant talking about lizards.

'Aye,' he was saying to the pink young man, 'they shed their tails. Drop them, when they're startled. When I was on the wards in Alexandria they used to play a game. There were always lizards skittering over the walls, you understand. Well, the game was to clap your hands when a lizard was just above the man in the bed opposite you so that it would drop its tail on him.'

'Really?' said the pink young man.

'What was that?' said the man from the Khedive's Office.

'He's telling him about the next torture,' said Paul. 'We keep these special lizards, and –'

'Really?' said the man from the Khedive's Office, looking thoughtful.

And it was just about then that the orderly came in to fetch Owen.

McPhee was waiting for him outside.

'Owen, there's been an attack at the Cut.'

'What on?'

'The dam, I think.'

'Any idea who by?'

McPhee hesitated.

'The Lizard Man, they say.'

He and Owen left at once. They found an arabeah in the Place Bab-el-Khalk with its driver sleeping beneath it, woke him and set out through the moonlit empty streets, with the domes and minarets mysterious against the velvety sky. It was about three in the morning and in another hour the city would be waking. Or, at least, some of it would. At the moment, however, there was nothing to impede them as the driver urged his horse along.

At the Cut men were stirring in the darkness but there were not the great crowds that Owen had feared. Selim came running excitedly towards them.

'Effendi, I have done it! I have killed the Lizard Man!'

'But, Selim –' began one of the other constables hesitantly.

'While these poofters were sleeping!' said Selim, dismissively. 'A Lizard Man has but a back like everyone else! That is what I said, didn't I, Abdul?'

'You did, Selim. But –'

'Then it can be broken like anyone else's back! That is what I said, didn't I?'

'You did. But, Selim –'

'And that is what I did. One blow, Effendi, that was all. But a mighty one!'

'I'm sure it was!'

'And there he lies, Effendi! Just the other side of the dam. I thought it best to leave him lest in his death agonies he might sweep me to the ground with his tail and fall upon me. That's what you've got to watch,' said Selim condescendingly, 'the tail. It is as with crocodiles. The tail is the most dangerous part. I know he is but a lizard, Effendi, but he's a hell of a big one!'

'How did it happen?' asked Owen.

'Well, Effendi,' said Selim, preening himself, 'I woke in the night and found I wanted to have a pee. So I prised myself loose from Amina's embraces – she is a dirty slut, I know, Effendi, and but a peanut seller, but when one is far from home one has to find consolation where one can – and went to water the canal bed. And then I thought: "I'll bet those idle sods are fast asleep!" For, Effendi, as guards they are not to be trusted. So I went to look, Effendi, for am I not Captain of the Guard?'

'You certainly are,' agreed Owen.

'Well, then. But, Effendi, I did not need to look for even from the bank I could hear Ibrahim's snores. "I will go over there," I said to myself, "and give that idle bastard a kick up the backside." But then, Effendi, I had a better idea. A really good one!'

'You did?'

'I thought, I will come upon him quietly, like a thief in the night. And I will lift his galabeeyah and bite him in the bum. And then he will think the Lizard Man has got him and shit hot bricks! That will teach the bugger to fall asleep when I am Captain of the Guard!'

'So, Effendi, I slid forward on my stomach like a lizard. And I had almost got there when I heard a noise, as of another lizard. And then I thought, it *is* another lizard! And then I thought, O, my God, it is the Lizard Man himself! Well, then, Effendi, I lay as one dead!

'And then I thought, Effendi, "He can have that stupid bastard, Ibrahim, for breakfast if he wants," and I began to slide away again.

'But then, Effendi, I stopped. Am I not Captain of the Guard, I said to myself? Am I the man to desert my post? And that stupid bastard, Ibrahim, asleep though he be? So, Effendi, I slid forward again and unshipped my truncheon.

'And there he was, Effendi, bold as brass, digging at the dam! Oh, ho, my beauty, I said to myself, we'll see about that! And I gave myself a really big swing and then landed him one right across the back. And he gave a great jump and a mighty groan and then lay still. But, Effendi, afterwards I did not go close for

167

I thought he might twitch. They do, you know. Crocodiles, that is. So –'

They came round the side of the dam.

'Bring a lamp!' said Owen.

'Selim –' said the hesitant constable again.

'What is it, Abdul? Why don't you go back to sleep? Now that all the real work has been done by others.'

'Selim, he is still alive!'

Owen lifted the lamp. By its light he could see a huddled figure lying against the face of the dam.

'Oh, is he? Stand aside, Effendi. Abdul, Ibrahim, get ready to rain blows upon him should he –'

'I don't think that will be necessary,' said Owen.

He could see now that the huddled form was that of a man. He went up to him and turned the body over with his foot.

'Why!' he said. 'It's –'

'Do you know him?' said McPhee.

'Oh, yes,' said Owen. 'It's one of the Muslim gravediggers.'

'He's broken my back!' groaned the gravedigger.

'That will teach you not to be the Lizard Man!' said Selim.

'Lizard Man?' said the gravedigger.

'You are a fortunate man,' said Owen. 'It could have been worse.'

'Lizard Man?' said the gravedigger, attempting to sit up. 'I don't want anything to do with the Lizard Man!'

'Leave him lying there!' said Owen. 'Let the Lizard Man take his own.'

'Here, look –' began the gravedigger.

'What were you doing there?' said Owen.

'Nothing!'

'Right, leave him!'

Owen began to walk away.

'Hey, wait!'

Owen turned.

'Well?'

'I was thinning out the dam,' said the gravedigger sulkily. 'In case those Jews get the job.'

'You were going to make the Cut yourself?'

'No, no. It'd take more than me to do that. No, I was just thinning it out in one place. So that it would fall on the Jews when they started.'

'That is a bad thing,' said Owen severely. 'Not only that, it is a stupid thing. What if you gain the contract?'

'We would know what to do.'

'Are the others with you on this?'

The gravedigger closed his mouth firmly.

'The contract goes to the Jews,' said Owen. 'You have brought this on your own head.'

By this time there was no point in going to bed. Owen was never able to sleep during the day. Instead, he went to the Bab-el-Khalk. Used though they were to his early ways, the bearers were surprised to see him.

At this time of the morning a night chill still hung over the building. To one fresh out from England, that pink young man, say, the temperature would have seemed pleasantly warm. Those longer in the sun thought of frost. Owen raised the jacket of his collar and huddled himself in his chair.

Fortunately, it was not long before he heard the pad of bare feet and smelled a delicious aroma and then Yussef, who had heard from the other orderlies that his master was in, appeared with coffee.

'Would the Effendi like me to send the barber in?' he suggested, seeing that Owen was unshaven.

'Why, yes!' said Owen.

'The Effendi was out all night?'

'Yes.'

'Down at the Cut?'

'Yes. For most of it.'

'I hope the charm worked,' said Yussef.

Owen sat up.

'Why, yes it did, Yussef! Yes, it did,' he said in surprise.

Restored, he felt able to contemplate his desk. Among the other messages, most of which appeared to be abusive ones from the Accounts Department, there was one from Georgiades. After some thought, and after the barber had visited, Owen put on his sun helmet and set out for the barrage.

The sun, now, was warming everything up, but out on the river, where there was a little breeze, the heat was not yet overpowering. On the left the misty, purple forms of the two great pyramids of Giza soared above the palm groves. On the right, outlined against the horizon, were the airy domes and flying minarets of the great mosque on the brow of Saladin's Citadel, lit up by the early morning sun.

Soon the barrage itself appeared up ahead, purple and rose in the sun. There was a crowd of people at the landing stage waiting for boats to take them in to the city. The felucca moved in past the water-carriers already filling their bags for the day's work.

Owen followed one of them up to the Gardens, past the sweet sellers and peanut sellers setting out their stalls, past the lemonade sellers top-heavy with their ornamental urns on their backs, and on through the trees towards the regulator.

Georgiades, alert this time, came to meet him. He led him through the bougainvillea to where the gardener was bent in a rose bed.

Georgiades walked forward and perched himself on the edge of a gadwal nearby. Owen stayed out of sight, but within hearing distance, behind the bougainvillea.

'You are about early!' said the gardener in surprise.

'I couldn't sleep,' said Georgiades.

'No?' said the gardener sympathetically. 'Well, it was hot last –'

'I was thinking of you,' said Georgiades.

'Of me?'

The gardener put down his trowel, staggered.

'I was saying to myself: he is my friend. Can I let him do it?'

'Do *what*?' said the gardener, beginning to get agitated.

'He is my friend. He had a wife, children. What will become of them when he is in the caracol?'

'In the caracol?'

'That's where you're going. I've heard them talking.'

'Allah!'

'They have found out, you see.'

'Found out?' said the gardener cautiously.

170

'About you and Ibrahim. And what you did to the bank the other day.'

The gardener sat stunned.

'Found out!' he whispered.

'Yes. There was no Lizard Man, was there? Just you and the ghaffir. You pulled out the stakes. You broke the Effendi's marking tape. And you broke away the bank to suggest that a beast had gone down to the canal to drink.'

'It was only in jest!' cried the gardener.

'Ah, but that was not how it seemed to the Effendi.'

'Yes, but –'

'Why did you do it, Abdullah? Why did you do a thing like that? You, who know so well the ways of water?'

'It was because of them! They were going to build a new canal. Right across my Gardens!'

'Did you think you could stop them, Abdullah? You, a mere gardener?'

'It was Ibrahim's idea! He said that now they knew there was a lizard man about, they would think it was him. He said that there had been much talk of lizard men lately, not just here but at the Cut. That the Effendi would think it was the same one, that it would make them pause and think –'

'They have paused, Abdullah, and they have thought. And they have alighted on you.'

'How did they come to alight on me?' whispered the gardener.

'They asked themselves who might wish to do a thing like that? And they remembered your concern for the Gardens. They asked who had the occasion to do it? And they thought of you and of Ibrahim. And they looked again at the place where the bank was breached and they saw not the marks of paws but the marks of a trowel.'

'What shall I do?' moaned the gardener.

'Well,' said Georgiades, 'if I were you, I would find some way of worming myself into the Mamur Zapt's graces.'

'How might I do that?'

Georgiades considered.

'You could start,' he considered, 'by telling him the name of the person to whom Babikr took the flowers.'

12

'Well, Babikr,' said Owen, 'now we know to whom it was you made your oath.'

'It was a bad oath,' said Babikr, looking at the ground. When he had been brought into Owen's office he had blinked at the light after more than a week in the cells.

'It was,' said Owen, 'and it was wrong of you to swear it.'

'I owed it to him. His family had helped mine when my wife was sick.'

'It is right to help neighbours. It is wrong to ask them to repay in wrong-doing.'

'I did not know that I would be asked to repay in that way. He and his family had left the village. Before they went, he came to me and said: "I know that you cannot repay me now what you owe me, and therefore I shall not ask it; but lest the debt you owe me be forgotten when you pay off your other debts I shall ask you to swear me an oath before the fiki."

'And I said:

' "It is true that I cannot repay you now, for all that I have earned has gone on my wife and child; but one day I shall repay it."

'And he said:

"I know you will. But still let us swear the oath."

'So we went to the fiki and when he heard what the oath was to be, he said: "That is not a good oath, for who knows its meaning?"

'And I said:

"Never mind if it is a good oath or not, that is the one he wants me to swear."

'Still the fiki demurred. But I was firm. "For," said I, "the man has helped my family when it was in need, and shall I now not repay him?"

'"Repay him, by all means," said the fiki, "but in money. For was not that what he lent you?"

'Well, I will not say that my heart was not troubled. But still I said: "I will swear as he wants, for am not I his debtor? And, besides, he says that a man may never be able to repay in money, but still he may repay in service. Even the poorest can repay in service."

'"Well, that is true," said the fiki, and so I swore the oath as he had asked.'

'What was the oath?'

'That when the time came for me to repay him, if he asked for service and not for money then I would be bound to offer him service; and that I would do whatsoever he demanded.'

'That was foolish!'

Babikr shrugged.

'So I see,' he said, 'now.'

'But did you not say so when you heard what he demanded?'

'I did. But he said: "I, too, am bound by an oath. An oath of revenge. I have sworn I will be revenged on him for what he has done to me. And now are you saying that I should break my oath as well as you break yours?" And I was troubled, for he had helped me freely when I was in need, and I had sworn freely. However I said to him: "You lent me money when I needed it – let me now give it back to you when you need it." For I could see that he had need. But he said: "The need I have is inside, and that is where you must repay me." But still, Effendi, I would not, and I left his house.

'But then I said to myself: "Babikr, have you not sworn? Did he not help you? And are you now saying that you will not help him?" So I went back to him and tried to reason with him. I said: "I came to you with joy in my heart that at last I could repay what I owed you. I came with flowers in my hand, wishing well to you and yours. But now that joy has turned to bitterness."

'"Well, then," he said, "it matches mine."

'I said: "This thing you wish to do is foolish as well as

wrong. For it will hurt not Al-Sayyid Hannam alone but everyone else."

'But he said:

'"I will revenge by water what was done by water. I will use the river to avenge what was done by the river."'

'Yes,' said the fiki. 'I remember the oath.'

'You did not remember it the other day,' said Owen.

'I hear many oaths.'

'From Babikr?'

The fiki was silent.

'Well,' he said at last, 'perhaps not from Babikr.'

'Did you not think? Knowing that the man was in prison?'

'I thought,' said the fiki, 'but I could not believe what I thought.'

So Owen went to the house of Ali Khedri; but he was not at home. That at first did not surprise him, for he supposed that the water-carrier would be out on his rounds. Then he saw, however, the water-skins thrown down in a corner and felt puzzled. He went to the neighbours and asked if they knew where Ali Khedri had gone, but they did not. He wondered if the water-carrier was over at Omar Fayoum's stable, helping the cart driver 'unharness the horses'. He and Georgiades began to make their way in that direction.

The building where Omar Fayoum kept his water-cart was empty. Of people, that was. The cart itself was there and there in a shed nearby which served as a stable were the horses. Which again was puzzling, for Omar was not a man to let his assets stand idle.

They walked round the building and came out at the back, where it crumbled away into the canal. A man, tarbooshed, dark-suited and perspiring, was picking his way gingerly along the bed. It was the manager from the Water Board; and this, too, was puzzling for in Cairo managers usually preferred the cool of their offices to the heat of the streets. He waved when he saw Owen and Georgiades and climbed up to meet them. He looked hot and bothered.

'You have not seen Suleiman?' he asked exasperatedly. 'I have been looking for him for the past hour. He is not supposed to be here at all. I did as you advised and ordered him out. He is supposed to be working in another district today and they are expecting him. But one of my people said that they had seen him over here!'

'And you came yourself?'

'Well, I was worried about him. After what you had said. And it was clearly no good sending anyone else!'

'He is disobeying instructions?'

'Yes. I had made it perfectly clear. I had him in yesterday and told him I was transferring him temporarily to the Hilmiya. He didn't like it. In fact, he begged me to let him stay, just for another day or two. Well, I remembered what you had said, and that a day or two would probably make no difference, but then I thought, no, if the boy is in danger, then he is in danger now, and what will his father think if I delay? So I told him firmly that he must transfer at once, that very day. He pleaded for just one more day, he said that he was on the brink of solving a problem that had been troubling us for months, that if I gave him just twenty-four hours –'

'But I said no, if he had information he could give us, then he would receive the credit for it but that he himself must start at once in the Citadel.'

'And yet today, you said, someone saw him here?'

'Yes.' The manager mopped his face with a large silk handkerchief. 'I don't mind telling you that I am very angry,' he said. 'He has been foolish, very foolish. And even though I am a friend of his father's –'

Owen interrupted him.

'This problem that you say he thought he was on the brink of solving: can you tell me what it was?'

'Yes. We have been concerned for some time that we have been losing water over here in the Rosetti. Now you always lose water, there is always a leaking pipe somewhere. But this was big and continuing. We were sure that someone was tapping the pipe. But what we could not understand was that it was the unfiltered water. Now if it had been the other pipe, the filtered water, that I could have understood, for the water there costs a lot more. But the unfiltered . . . It comes straight from the river. We don't do anything to it and so it is dirt cheap. It would hardly be worth anyone's while –'

'Just a minute,' said Owen; 'you say you think someone was tapping it? And that Suleiman was on the brink of finding out who it was?'

'So he said.'

'And it was here in the Gamaliya?'

'Somewhere over here. In the Rosetti, more likely. We haven't really gone into the Gamaliya yet.'

'Then I think,' said Owen, 'that I am beginning to understand. And I think we should try to find him quickly!'

The workman had reported seeing Suleiman near the Khan-el-Khalil. The manager had gone there first and luckily found someone who remembered seeing Suleiman that morning. From there he had followed his trail along the Sikkel-el-Gedida to the Place-el-Kanto. In the *souk* there he had talked to an onion seller who had pointed him on towards the Khalig Canal. There he had hesitated for a while but then, remembering that the Water Board's pipes ran along the bank of the canal at one point, had nobly set off along the bed.

'Right,' said Owen. 'Now, you go to the police station, as fast as you can, and tell them that the Mamur Zapt needs men. At once!'

The manager set off. Georgiades, meanwhile, had run along the canal bank to where a donkey was cropping the greenery that stretched down into the canal bed. Not far away, as he had suspected, its owner was stretched out in the shade. He came hurrying back.

'The boy came along here less than an hour ago. He was looking around him. At the banks, the man says. He says he climbed out of the canal about here and went in among the houses.'

They began to walk along the Sharia Ben-es-Suren, Georgiades taking the streets on the left, Owen the little alleyways leading down to the Canal on the right. In one of them he saw some women chatting at a fountain with pitchers balanced on their heads.

'I am looking for a boy,' he said urgently. 'Leila's friend. Have you seen him?'

'Suleiman?'

The word passed round. People began to join them in the search. Two of them brought a match seller along who claimed to have seen him.

'Which way?'

The man pointed towards the canal. Owen plunged in that direction. This part of the city, one of the oldest, was like a warren. Streets gave onto streets, alleyway into alleyway. They became narrower and narrower, mere tunnels beneath the walls. They turned in on themselves, back on themselves.

Emerging, to his surprise, on to a street he had already canvassed, he saw with relief the manager returning with policemen from the local station; with Mahmoud, too.

'I was at the station when he came,' he said. 'I wanted a constable. But your need seems greater than mine.'

He disappeared with the constables into the alleyways.

Owen went back towards the canal. That at least was a thread of direction. He tried to keep going alongside it but some of the streets ended before they quite reached it and blocks of houses, tiny and ramshackle, were forever intervening. In this labyrinth a man could easily disappear: for ever.

In the distance he thought he heard a shriek.

Another block. He descended into the canal in order to get round it. As he climbed up the other side he saw a man waving urgently.

'Effendi! Effendi!'

At the end of the street he saw Georgiades. There was a woman beside him, collapsed on the ground, rocking herself to and fro in the posture of grief. He ran towards them.

The woman looked up at him. The tear-stained face was that of Um Fatima.

'They went out to look for him!' she moaned.

'Ali Khedri?'

'And Uthman!'

'Which way?'

'I do not know. He seized his knife and ran out. I tried to hold him back. "Have you not done enough?" I said. But he

177

thrust me aside. "Out of the way, woman!" he said. "This touches us all!" '

She began to rock more violently. Women rushed up to her and tried to comfort her. Some began to keen in sympathy.

Owen looked frantically around him. Minute alleyways ran away on every side.

The Water Board manager was standing there bewildered.

'The pipes!' said Georgiades. 'Where are they?'

The manager looked at him mutely. Georgiades took him by the lapels and shook him. 'The pipes! Where do they come out?'

'Further up!' whispered the manager. 'In the canal. Further up!'

Georgiades jumped down into the canal bed and began running.

'You can get there more quickly through the houses,' said the manager, recovering.

'Show me!'

He gave the man a push and he started running. Confidently at first, doubling through the houses, plunging unhesitatingly through the alleyways, but then, after one double too many, more slowly. Owen raced after him.

'This one!' he said, making for a narrow snick, almost invisible in the shadow.

They ran down it and emerged high up on the bank of the canal. To their left was a mass of crumbling fretwork, the remains of some old meshrebiya windows, covered now with creeper and weed, the heavy corbels that had once supported them still jutting out from the wall; to their right, the canal bent round a corner and just out of sight Owen could hear urgent, scrambling footsteps. Georgiades came into sight, panting.

'It must be further up,' said the manager doubtfully.

Owen cursed and dropped down into the bed in a shower of stones. Georgiades ran past without speaking. Owen caught up with him where a fall had spread rubble along the bed for perhaps twenty yards and where they had to pick their way over crumbling bricks and huge, rotting baulks of timber.

He knew now where they were. Ahead of him were the old Mameluke houses, with their picturesque balconies and great, protruding, box-like windows, built to look down on a canal which had been the glory of the Old City, now frail and crumbling, hanging on to the houses by a thread.

A stone landed at his feet. He looked up and saw the stone-throwing small boy of the other day. The stone, though, this time, was thrown less in hostility than as a declaration of identity.

'Where are they?' he called urgently.

The boy pointed up beyond the houses.

'Is he there?'

'They have him.'

He tried to find a burst of speed but they had come now to a place where the rubble had given way to mud in which their feet sank and kept sticking.

'You are faster than I,' he called to the boy. 'Run on and shout that the Mamur Zapt is coming!'

It might lose them the men; but it might save Suleiman.

The boy hesitated.

'They will kill me,' he said.

'They will reward you. And I will reward you too!'

The boy set off, scrabbling along the bank, his bare feet finding a purchase where their shoes could not.

They heard him shout.

Owen hurled himself on, his feet sticking now on slime-covered slabs of stone that had fallen out of the steps leading down from the old, decaying houses.

There was a bend in the canal and now, emerging from the bank and leading along the side of it, he could see pipes.

He came fully round the bend and then there, ahead of him, he saw them: four figures, Suleiman, high up on a terrace, hammering desperately on a door, and three men, Ali Khedri, Ahmed Uthman and the cart driver, advancing up the steps towards him.

Owen and Georgiades ran forward. The cart driver, knife in hand, dropped back to meet them.

'Help me, Ali!' he called back over his shoulder. 'Leave it to Ahmed!'

Ali Khedri took no notice.

'Ali!'

179

'I want to do it,' said Ali Khedri; and began to move up the steps.

The cart driver cursed and fell back to the bottom of the steps. 'Come down here, you fool!' he called. 'This needs two of us. One will do for him!'

Ali Khedri wavered, dropped down a step and then stood there undecided.

Ahmed Uthman took a length of cord out from under his galabeeyah and ran up on to the terrace.

Suleiman left the door and ran to the end of the terrace. Above him was a huge box-like meshrebiya window, so huge even by Mameluke standards that at some time in the past it had been found necessary to support it by putting two posts beneath it.

Suleiman looked around desperately and then began to climb up one of the posts.

Ahmed Uthman ran forward and tried to catch him by the leg. Suleiman kicked his hand away and climbed further, up to where he could reach the window. There, though, he came to a stop. Every time he reached for a new hand-hold, the worm-eaten fretwork crumbled away.

Ahmed Uthman began to climb up the post towards him.

Back along the terrace the door suddenly burst open and Mahmoud came through, followed by a group of constables.

'Enough!' he shouted, running along the terrace. 'Enough!'

The cart driver, distracted, looked towards the shout. Georgiades hit him hard behind the ear. He fell back on to the steps and the knife dropped from his hand.

Owen had reached Ali Khedri. He caught him by the galabeeyah and swung him round. He came down the steps to Georgiades, who hit him as he came.

Up on the terrace, though, Ahmed Uthman had nearly reached Suleiman.

Suleiman made another despairing grab. A large piece of fretwork came away in his hand. The whole structure began to totter. Up above, there was a tearing sound as the woodwork detached itself from the wall.

'Get hold of the supports!' shouted Mahmoud. 'Get hold of the supports!'

The window collapsed in a great cloud of dust. For a moment or two they could not see anything; and then there was Suleiman still above them, somehow clinging to one of the massive corbels that had once supported the huge, protruding window.

Suleiman was able to show them the place. It was a little further along the canal, where the fine old Mameluke mansions gave way to lower, humbler ones, some of them derelict, others occupied, rather than rented out, as workshops. Omar Fayoum had taken over one of them as a place, he said, to store gear for his horses and the water-cart. It had the added advantage of a cellar right next to the bank of the canal.

The pipes of the Water Board disappeared at this point, not so much underground as into a mass of debris. Most of it came from adjoining houses which had collapsed into the bed long ago but some of it was new and it was this that had drawn Suleiman's attention to the place. Clambering over the wreckage, he had seen signs of recent working about the pipes which had aroused his suspicions. He had attached flow measuring gauges on either side of the spot and been able to establish that on occasion substantial quantities of water were illicitly drawn off.

He had guessed that the pipe was some how being tapped from the premises above but it had taken him some time to work out, first, that the house must have a cellar, through which the pipes could be reached, and then that it belonged to Omar Fayoum.

Once, though, he had made the connection with the water-seller, things began to fall into place. He had observed that the water-cart called regularly at the house to an extent hardly likely to be justified by the pretext that it was picking up gear. He had found that it was clearly picking up water and had followed it afterwards to the various points at which it disbursed it to the local water-carriers.

Still, though, there were things that he could not understand. The greatest of these was the economics of it. The water that was being stolen was unfiltered water. True, it was then being sold as filtered water, fit for drinking, but even so the mark up must be minute. It was only gradually that he realized that to men like these the margin, however small, was significant. Where a man's dreams of wealth turned on the difference between being a water-carrier and a man on a cart, milliemes mattered.

In Omar Fayoum's case the profit margin was greater anyway because the bulk of the water was sold as drinking water to businesses – cafés, for instance – in the Gamaliya which the pipes had not yet reached.

Suleiman had not known this, had not known any of it, in the days when he had hung around the Gamaliya desperate for a sight of Leila. But Omar Fayoum, and the men about him, knowing his business in the Gamaliya, and forever seeing him there, 'creeping around', as they put it, had suspected that he did.

When, therefore, his connection with Leila had become known, it was like a thunderbolt. Surely he would be able to worm the secret out of her; and if by then she was married to Omar Fayoum, it would be even worse.

The marriage was called off at once; and to the collapse of Ali Khedri's hopes in that respect was added the fear that the whole scheme was on the verge of being discovered.

And by the son of his old enemy! This was the bit that Ali Khedri could not bear. Nor could he believe that it had come about by accident. To his diseased mind it was clear that his old adversary was pursuing him further, even here in the city, even here in the depths of his poverty.

He had to hit back. And he had to hit back before time ran out, before they came and took him to a place where he might be able to think about revenge but would never be able to take it. He had to hit back; and to a man whose life was water, whose life, as he saw it, had been ruined by water, water was the obvious means by which to take his revenge. He would use the river, as Babikr had said, to avenge what was done by the river.

Babikr had come to him as a gift from God; or, possibly, – and by this time he did not care – from Shaitun. He had called on Ali Khedri when he had come up to do his annual duty with the corvée. He knew the barrage and, even more

182

to the point, was bound, as he had reminded Ali Khedri, to him by oath.

For Ali Khedri, as for Suleiman, things were falling into place. Babikr might demur, but he was bound. Ali Khedri thanked God or Shaitun for the terms of the oath on which he had insisted. About the effect on others of his taking revenge in this way on his old adversary, he did not care. All else was consumed in the bitterness he felt for Al-Sayyid Hannam.

And then it did not work. Babikr planted the bomb, the Manufiya Regulator was blown, but Al-Sayyid Hannam, though damaged, was not broken.

He even had the gall to come to him, him, Ali Khedri, whom he had wronged so badly, asking – this was rich, so rich that it could not be chance, it must be cunning – for forgiveness.

So back they were to things as they had been, with his old enemy triumphant, even, it seemed, on the verge of a greater triumph. For there could be no mistake about it now. The boy had found out. He had attached his infernal devices to the pipes on either side of the tap and that meant, Omar Fayoum said, that he would be able to show that there was no doubt about it.

Unless, of course, he was stopped.

And then they heard that the boy was again in the Gamaliya, there, at the very spot!

It was their last chance to save themselves. More than that; for Ali Khedri it was another chance, and, yes, again, probably his last chance, to get even with his old adversary. For Al-Sayyid Hannam loved his boy. The man from the Parquet had said so. Loved him. Perhaps this, not the water, was the way to find revenge.

'You sought revenge,' said Owen coldly, 'through harming innocence.'

'Innocence? You call the boy innocent?'

'He was but doing his job.'

Ali Khedri was unconvinced.

'He was put up to it,' he said, 'by his father.'

'And what of those others whom you would have harmed along with Al-Sayyid Hannam?'

The water-carrier shrugged.

'Some of them came from your village. They remembered you in friendship. They will not do that now. They will think of you with anger. As a man who would have hurt his friends. And as a man who killed his daughter.'

Ali Khedri started up.

'I did not kill her!' he cried.

'No,' said Mahmoud, speaking for the first time. Up till now he had been sitting there quietly, for the attack on the regulator was Owen's business. Leila, however, was his. 'No, you did not kill her. But I think you know who did.'

Ali Khedri started to say something, stopped and looked at the ground.

'You must have guessed,' said Mahmoud. 'Even if he did not speak of it when you left the meeting together, you must have guessed when you heard that Leila had not come back.'

'She was nothing to do with me,' said Ali Khedri defiantly.

'She was your daughter. Even though others had taken her in. And that was sad, that Um Fatima, who in the goodness of her heart had taken her in, should by that same act make it possible for her to be killed. For surely she would not have gone with Ahmed Uthman if she had not come from his house and trusted him.'

'She would have gone with any man,' said Ali Khedri.

'Not so. For she was pure in heart. She would not have gone with the boy. There were two men only that she would have gone with: her father and the man who in her trustfulness she thought was acting as her father. He had taken her in and had a right to tell her to come with him.'

The water-carrier was silent.

'Let me take you back, Ali Khedri,' said Mahmoud, 'to the afternoon of the day that Leila died, when you and Ahmed Uthman and Omar Fayoum talked for so long in the place where Omar Fayoum kept his cart; when all that you knew was that the boy might be close to discovering your secret about the water and that he loved the girl; and when you were still brooding in your heart upon the fresh wrong that you fancied your old adversary, Al-Sayyid Hannam, had done you and meditating your revenge by water. What I want to know is this: when you and Ahmed Uthman and

184

Omar Fayoum talked for so long, did you talk about kill-ing Leila?'

He waited, but the water-carrier did not reply.

'You were, I think, talking about the boy and what he had found out. And I suspect you talked about what you might do. Did that include killing your daughter?'

Ali Khedri remained mute.

'You would have feared that she would tell what she knew.'

'She knew nothing,' said Ali Khedri, speaking at last.

'Why, then, was the marriage with Omar Fayoum broken off?'

'Because of what she might find out.'

'Yet she had not found it out when she was living with you?'

'A daughter's duty is to obey,' said Ali Khedri.

'And you thought a wife might not?'

'Her heart was with the boy.'

'You thought she would betray you?'

'I do not know,' muttered Ali Khedri.

'Did you talk about that?'

'I don't know what we talked about.'

'I ask,' said Mahmoud, 'for this reason: Uthman will die. You probably will die, too. Shall Omar Fayoum escape? Do the rich always go free in this world?'

13

One thing remained: to see that on the great day there was no trouble between Jews and gravediggers. Owen found the gravediggers sitting disconsolately in the shade of a tomb.

'The Jews are doing it,' they said.

'It was their turn,' said Owen. 'And, besides, you have brought it on your own heads.'

'It was his idea,' one of them tried. 'Why are you taking it out on us?'

'You knew about it,' said Owen.

They did not really demur.

'However,' said Owen, 'I am a man of mercy.'

'You are?'

They looked up hopefully.

'Yes. And therefore although the Jews will still do it –'

Gravedigger faces fell.

'– I will put in a word for you on a job that will be more than equivalent.'

'What is that?' asked the gravediggers cautiously.

'You know that after the Cut, the canal is to be filled in. For that, diggers will be required. It is a good job and will last many days. Now, I will see that you get the chance to do half; provided that I have no more trouble from you.'

'Half the canal? That will take a bit of time. The usual rates?'

'Certainly.'

'Well, that's not bad!' said one of them.

'In fact, it's very good,' said another.

The gravediggers brightened.

'Remember, only if I have no trouble!' Owen cautioned.

'Who is doing the other half?'

'The Jews.'

There was a long silence. Then one of the men said:

'It would be the other end from us, wouldn't it?'

'Yes.'

'You'd have to see that they didn't do a bit of our half sneakily and then claim for it.'

'I would see to that,' Owen promised. 'I will get the Effendi from the barrage to measure – he measures like the Prophet himself! – and determine the mid-point, so that there will be no arguing. And then I shall watch like a hawk to see that neither half – neither half! – is exceeded.'

'We-ell . . .' said the gravediggers, looking at each other.

'We'll have to think about it.'

'Don't think too long!'

'Are you talking to the Jews too?'

Owen nodded.

'We're on!' said the gravediggers instantaneously.

'But will the Lizard Man strike?' asked the man from the Khedive's Office worriedly.

'There is no such thing as the Lizard Man,' said Owen wearily, very wearily because on top of the excitements of the previous day he had been up most of the night checking last minute arrangements for the Cut, marshalling boats, reinforcing the police cordon, making sure that the canal bed was clear of idiots who were determined to drown themselves, and pacifying the Kadi, the Khedive, the Consul-General's wife, and Zeinab, who had decided after a couple of hours that there were better things to do with one's nights than standing around on a dam and wanted Owen to do them with her.

'I heard there had been incidents,' said the man from the Khedive's Office uneasily.

'You heard wrongly,' said Owen shortly.

'There was that attack on the Manufiya Regulator –'

'The men responsible are in prison. And they are men not lizards.'

'Oh, I know about that. But wasn't there something else?'

'A foolish attempt by a gardener and a ghaffir to stop the new canal from running through the Gardens!'

'And there was an attempt to disrupt the Cut itself!'

'There were two incidents. Neither was by a lizard. One was probably by a stray dog and the other certainly by an astray gravedigger who now languishes in jail.'

'But there was this business about the girl –'

'Nothing to do with it. An unconnected murder.'

'But the body, I understand, was found beneath the Cone?'

'Put there by a killer to distract attention and throw suspicion on someone else. You may assure His Royal Highness that there is no danger. From the Lizard Man or anything else.'

'I hope so,' said the man from the Khedive's Office doubtfully. He, too, had had a hard night manoeuvring his master's barge into a position which offered the best possible view but would keep him out of the way should anything go wrong with the tricky business of the Cut itself. The Khedive had at one time wanted to be the one whose boat made the actual breach and it had been very difficult to persuade him that that was traditionally the Kadi's prerogative. His Highness had been convinced only when it was pointed out to him that the first boat through was the one that had to ride the turbulence.

The Kadi himself had no need to be reminded of this fact.

'Just make sure the damned thing doesn't turn over!' he kept saying; although his was not, in fact, the boat that would be making the actual breach. Tucked out of sight beneath the bows of the Kadi's barge was a smaller vessel which would be sent on ahead, its crew shivering in their sandals.

The river side of the dam was now a solid mass of boats jostling for position. When the dam was broken they would follow the Kadi through in a joyous and noisy convoy. Some would certainly sink, and the most that Owen could hope for was that they would sink far enough along the Canal not to disrupt proceedings. Fortunately, they had all done this lots of times before and knew what was expected of them.

He checked the earth dam for the last time. The Jews had done their work, shaving the wall of the dam to the point where a boat could crash through it, and were now standing resting on their wooden spades.

'Okay,' said Owen. 'Get them away!'

The police closed round them and hustled them out of sight.

There had been no trouble. The Muslim gravediggers were sticking to the deal.

Macrae was standing nearby with a bottle in his hand. He held it out to Owen.

'Have a wee drappie!' he invited. 'It's a cauld night!'

Well, by Egyptian standards it was. Owen accepted gratefully. From along the river bank came the skirl of pipes; bag, not water.

'It's the Camerons!' cried Macrae.

Not so; into sight came a native Egyptian band, complete with drums, cymbals, hautboys, oods, nays – and bagpipes.

'Canna ye tell the Camerons, man?' said Ferguson, scandalized.

'Ay, but –' said Macrae, puzzled. Then: 'Look at the pipes!' he cried. They were genuine Scottish bagpipes, still covered with the tartans of the clans they had served.

'All the music shops have them,' said Owen, taking another swig.

'Just cut out the drink!' advised Zeinab, appearing with Labiba Latifa. 'You know you'll be useless!'

'I must thank you for your efforts on behalf of Suleiman, Captain Owen,' said Labiba, smiling. 'Now, about circumcision –'

'I have been talking to Mahmoud about it,' said Owen hurriedly. 'He's just over there, I believe.'

'Is he?'

Labiba plunged into the crowd. Zeinab stayed to address him; forthrightly, it appeared, from the emphaticness of her gestures. However he couldn't hear a word because at that moment the Kadi's barge fired off its cannon. Immediately there were answering sallies from the barges round about and drums began to beat on all the smaller boats. Rockets whizzed into the sky. Humbler fireworks began to crackle along the banks of the canal, their sparks and stars illuminating the faces of the onlookers.

In a momentary lull he heard a familiar voice.

'But I *did* see him!' it insisted.

It was the man from the Khedive's Office, this time in company with Paul.

'I am sure you did,' replied Paul soothingly.

'But you said he was being tortured!'

'I did, yes.'

'You spoke of some Glass House!'

'Well, yes.'

'And now he is here!'

'Ah, yes,' said Paul, 'but it is what he is here *for*.'

'What is he here for?'

Paul glanced around and then took him conspiratorially by the arm.

'You see that mound of earth?'

'The Bride of the Nile, yes.'

'Well, that's it.'

'You are going to put him there?'

'Spread-eagled. So that he can see the water coming towards him.'

'They are usually killed first,' said the man from the Khedive's Office doubtfully.

'Yes, but it's better this way, don't you think?'

'Well, yes. I suppose so. But, look, it's usually a woman. They're best for this kind of thing.'

'I agree with you entirely. It was just that in this case I thought – you know, considering what he had done: the insult to the Khedive, the connection with the river –'

'Using the river to punish for the river?' said the Khedive's man, impressed. 'Well, yes, that is imaginative. I will go and tell His Royal Highness to look out for it as his boat goes through. He probably won't see anything, but –'

He hurried away. Paul seized Macrae by the arm.

'Have you got some whisky?'

'Why, yes, man,' said Macrae hospitably, offering him the bottle.

'No, no. You see that chap there?'

He pointed to the pink young man.

'Yes. He's my assistant.'

'It should be easy, then. Look, what I want him to do is drink half a bottle –'

'Half a bottle! But –'

'These are instructions from the Consul-General,' said Paul impressively. 'The new Manufiya Regulator depends on it!'

190

'It does?'

Macrae shrugged his shoulders in bewilderment but strode purposefully towards the pink young man.

Paul caught Owen's eye and mock wiped his brow.

'Now where the hell's the Consul-General's Lady got to?' he said, and slipped away.

The band had reached the dam now and, undaunted by the competition, were giving a last mighty blow.

'Owen,' said McPhee, 'have you remembered?'

'Remembered?'

'The indecency. The licentiousness.'

'Well –'

'Only Her Ladyship is just arriving.'

'I think she's too early. It hasn't begun yet.'

There was a sudden, deafening blare of trumpets. The flotilla beyond the dam began to move. The Kadi was coming!

The din was deafening. Rockets lit the sky in a continuous explosion. Tars clashed, darabukhas drummed. The pipers beside the dam pumped frantically.

From beneath the bows of the Kadi's barge a small boat shot out and headed for the dam.

The Kadi stood up to read his proclamation, inaudible in the uproar.

And then suddenly you could hear him. The tumult was cut off. The small boat was approaching the dam. The Kadi paused.

The small boat hit the wall and stuck for a moment. There was a concerned gasp from the crowd. But then the specially pointed bows were thrusting forward, the earth on either side falling away, and a great wave of water rushing forward into the canal.

It hit the Bride and dissolved her in an instant. On the banks people began capering in ecstasy.

In a moment the canal was full and the water pouring on downstream. The Kadi's barge hit the remains of the earth dam, seemed to stick for a second and then surged triumphantly through.

The Khedive's barge burst through after it, and then a whole line of boats began to come through the gap, their occupants dancing, waving excitedly to the crowds, letting off fireworks and banging every utensil in sight.

On the banks now there was continuous uproar. Musicians were beating the darabukhas frantically. The pipes were piping fit to burst. Almost at once, everyone was dancing.

Over to his right Owen caught sight of Selim at the head of a long line, snaking, or, possibly, lizarding in and out of the cake and sweetmeat stalls. All at once he darted into the crowd and reemerged with a buxom lady, his hands on her hips, at first, and then elsewhere.

'Owen,' said McPhee agitatedly, 'do you think this is entirely suitable?'

On the banks people were stripping off their clothes and diving into the water. Women were brazenly showing off their faces and – was not that an indecent arm? Veils, decency, all was discarded. Well, yes, in some cases, all.

'Owen,' began McPhee.

But Zeinab came dancing up and plucked the Mamur Zapt away.

'Owen,' tried McPhee again, following them, 'do you think this is entirely suitable?'

'Oh, yes,' said Owen over Zeinab's shoulder. 'Entirely.'

'I do feel Her Ladyship –'

But Her Ladyship herself came dancing by at that moment with the surprised but ever-adaptable Paul held firmly in her grasp.

'Dead?' said a familiar voice.

'Well, what do you think?' said Paul, disengaging himself from Her Ladyship and passing her on deftly to the man from the Khedive's Office. He came and stood beside Owen, who had lost Zeinab for the moment. She had seen Labiba and Mahmoud talking together very seriously and had decided to help her in going in for the kill.

The two men stood for a moment looking down at the Canal bobbing with boats and swimmers and including now in its embraces Selim, entirely divested of his uniform and hot in pursuit of a lady similarly unencumbered.

'Lizard Man meets Nile Maiden,' said Paul affectionately.